Prai

Roxy and Coco

"Existing at the sweet spot between Rachel Ingalls's *Mrs. Caliban*, Donald Barthelme's *Snow White*, and James Purdy's *I Am Elijah Thrush*, *Roxy and Coco* plucks a creature out of myth to bring it into our present—and does so in a way that keeps a steady eye on the flaws of our own weird moment. Rarely has fantastic fiction managed to say so much so deftly about the real while still offering a terrific, strange, and highly original read."

—Brian Evenson, author of *Song for the Unraveling of the World*

"There are many mythic reimaginings out there, but I can guarantee you that *Roxy and Coco* is unlike anything you've read—Terese Svoboda's harpies are winged avengers, a celestial task force who save kids who have been abused by their terrestrial protectors. Who but Svoboda with her talons descending from the clouds could wrest so much humor, poetry, and beauty from the abyss?"

—Karen Russell, author of *Orange World* and *Swamplandia!*

Roxy and Coco

A Novel

TERESE SVOBODA

WEST VIRGINIA UNIVERSITY PRESS · MORGANTOWN

"Victory," from *Fox: Poems 1998–2000* by Adrienne Rich. Copyright © 2001 by
Adrienne Rich. Used by permission of W. W. Norton & Company, Inc.

ISBN 978-1-959000-06-8 (paperback) / 978-1-959000-07-5 (ebook)

Library of Congress Cataloging-in-Publication Data
Names: Svoboda, Terese, author.
Title: Roxy and Coco : a novel / Terese Svoboda.
Description: First edition. | Morgantown : West Virginia University Press, 2024.
Identifiers: LCCN 2023040795 | ISBN 9781959000068 (paperback) | ISBN
     9781959000075 (e-book)
Subjects: LCSH: Sisters—Fiction. | Harpies (Greek mythology)—Fiction. |
     LCGFT: Novels.
Classification: LCC PS3569.V6 R69 2024 | DDC 813/.54—dc23/eng/20230905
LC record available at https://lccn.loc.gov/2023040795

Book and cover design by Than Saffel / WVU Press
Cover image licensed by Science History Images / Alamy Stock Photo

for JoAnn

the Nike of Samothrace
on a staircase   wings in blazing
backdraft   said to me
: : to everyone she met
           Displaced, amputated   never discount me
           —"Victory," Adrienne Rich

And Thaumas wedded Electra the daughter of deep-
flowing Ocean, and she bore him swift Iris and the
     long-haired
Harpies, Aello (Coco-swift) and Ocypetes (Swift-flier)
     who on
their swift wings keep pace with the blasts of the winds
     and the
birds; for quick as time they dart along.
           —*Theogony 267*, Hesiod

They have wings and claws because love flies and
     wounds.
           —*Etymologies,* Book 11, Isidore of Seville

Human DNA contains all the necessary genes to
     produce feathers—it's merely a matter of selective
     activation.
           —Weird Science tweet @weird_sci, June 30, 2021

ROXY AND COCO

Chapter 1

I LIKE the way *harpy* sounds—it has a kind of harp-like angelic appeal, the music of heaven. Otherwise we don't have any closer connection to the spiritual than a Fats Waller recording on a Sunday. If humans catch us gliding overhead, a whoosh of beak and feather and claw, why, it keeps them alert, and the distraction might stop them from killing each other for a few minutes. So maybe we are angels, whoever they are. Except for the violence I find myself drawn to. Roxy's a little more patient than I am and tries to rein me in, but it's not much use—I'm attracted to certain unsavory practices.

Coco, Coco, she says, you have to rethink this.

And it's only been a week.

I bang my way into the house and the baby we're supposed to pick up is lying across the radiator. I mean, he's wedged between the wall and the top of the radiator, the steam around him visible. Despite the heat, his top half is blue, he's half-frozen, being naked, and there's pee dripping to the floor. Of course he's crying. Maybe in some drug-induced haze the parents thought this was the only way to keep him warm? I pick him up and he's got hatch marks up his back where the skin is singed. I played with this kid for an hour yesterday. He likes peekaboo, he likes tickling.

I balance him backward on my hip and take a cell phone picture of the burns. Evidence. I find a shirt lying around and wrap him in it. Not tight. He screams worse now but he has to stay warm. I should bring him out to the van right away but I don't, I follow the music. It blares, concert loud, from a speaker in the room at the end of the hall where I find the parents, asleep fully dressed—correction, half-dressed, the girl not quite on the bed.

I take another picture. The baby's crying gets fierce, almost drowns out the music. Nobody stirs.

I step into the center of the room and shrug off my jacket so my wings—span eight feet, tipped with claws—cut off the window light.

The baby in my arms stops crying.

I hiss.

The girl opens her eyes, takes one look at me, and screams. The guy is up on his feet, scuffling back against the wall.

I cut the music.

What's the problem? Stewie shouts from the front door. We've got three more stops.

I hiss again. She says she's seeing things. Hallucinations.

Be right there, says Stewie, coming down the hall.

My wings *zzzt* like a convertible closing between my shoulders, my jacket's back on by the time he walks in. The baby starts up again. I must've jostled him. Careful, he's burned, I say, but he quiets the second Stewie takes him.

He gives the parents the once-over.

I saw something, the girl protests. She is pointing at me, her arm shaking. *Dazed* is not a strong enough word—the guy's jaw covers his Adam's apple.

We have to get the baby to Emergency, I say. These two are nuts.

No, no—really, both of us saw her, she says. The baby's crying obliterates whatever the guy's saying.

We've got to go, says Stewie.

The girl is now wagging her head as if to clear it.

Drunk and psychotic, I say. Write that down. Maybe that will get the kid a better deal.

Chapter 2

ROXY'S ACCUMULATION of glitter displayed on her bureau—always with the sparkly wrapping paper, aluminum pop-tops, sequins—is stunning. She's just tossed her bracelet into the mix, whistling to Spotify.

I'm perched at the edge of her bed. I don't get it. Why not take the kids away?

If both parents are together, they're hard to beat out of custody. It's not usually so bad.

Twice as bad with the Collinses, is what I think. I pick up my mug and blow over it.

Roxy's wings, like our deceased mother's, almost touch the ceiling. She gives them an impatient flap. It's good to have you back.

You can't always be doing this SOS thing.

I'm always hoping we've evolved so far that it will work out.

Is that why you weren't here last night? I take a sip of tea. Working late.

I'll bet.

She shoves a drawer closed with her hip, she grins. He likes to work.

We'll get to him, I laugh. Why do they call it respite child care? I think it's despite child care.

More like desperate, if you ask me. The court doesn't offer respite all the time. Her voice is muffled, her head's in her armpit, she's preening. It's just when they put on a big show and the court says okay, get yourselves together, and this is how we'll help keep the family going. Look, it's not like they can put parents in stocks anymore.

That was such a good idea. I sigh and close my eyes. I can't believe social services these days has so many rules. You had my job for a whole year?

I learned to hold my temper, she says. I don't have to look into the eyes of abandoned kids anymore, just the culprits. Uncurling and curling her long fingers, she's doing the dinosaur thing with her neck, bobbing around, and not to the music.

Please, I say.

She stops with the bobbing and drinks her tea. She's so blonde and calm, people think she's an angel but when she's pushed, her temper's definitely on par with mine. Being so dark, at least hair-wise, people act like I'm the scary one. I can be scary, but I can wear red lipstick, and do glamor. Harpies have a bad rap about their looks, but it's strictly a projection of fear from male content providers. Even today, when no one thinks of us outside of fifth-grade classics-lite lessons, every wiki insists we are ugly, winged women entwined with poisonous serpents.

We hate snakes.

I fling myself across the covers. I'm tired from flying all the way from Europe. Harpies are not really so immortal, our genes are just slow at signaling No. We get old. I may look like a college girl but my feathers are no longer so glossy. I have to wash my wings. This lack of true immortality is why we continue to lay eggs.

Roxy's filing her nails.

You know, the French give out money for childcare, I say, but kids still get hurt. Same rate as here. Money never fixes anything.

My last case told me it was better to be beaten than to be left alone. She screws her cold cream closed. You lost the accent pretty fast.

I imitate a Senegalese cabbie. I imitate a Manchurian pony handler. I imitate Eleanor Roosevelt.

She groans.

So when do I get to meet him?

You already have, she says, her face both sly and happy, fluttering in place. I thought for sure you'd figure out who it was right away.

It's not so easy anymore.

Well? She wraps a robe around herself.

He certainly knows how to fold his wings nicely, if it's Tim, the guy in charge.

Roxy shrugs. Maybe he's had surgery. Just passing him down the hall—

She splays her fingers as if she's just touched a socket.

I plump up her pillow. It would be great if he were harpy, I concede. But today I heard him threatening to take a child away because the father gave her a diet coke for breakfast. He's like that?

Roxy looks up from the computer she's now got propped on her knees. She says, not very convincingly, he's just being zealous.

Maybe he gets a bonus for every child he puts up for adoption. Just guessing, I say when the look she gives me threatens annihilation.

He's complicated, she says, and goes off in a huff to brush her teeth, calling out over the running water: I just like the idea of a guy sticking around.

I'm silent, the best I can do after such a remark. Roxy's interest in romance is awfully human. With harpies, there's none of that dancing around like other birds when they mate, and is there ever any hand-holding afterward, any split-the-rent-and-save-up-for-the-kid's-college? Nope, none of the love stuff. Romance is messy and time-consuming and irrational; instinct is automatic. Ba-boom. Over. The male harpy swoops down and tups us from behind, then he's gone. That makes them hard to ID, even for us.

By the time Rox finishes her bedtime routine, I've packed our lunches for tomorrow: fizzy water, sunflower seeds, a little bar of suet I bought that looks just like an energy bar. It is an energy bar. Make him eat an avocado, I say, that'll tell you if he's a harpy.

I want him dead? she screeches. Anyway—she takes a deep breath—I tried that a week ago. He said he was allergic.

Tim, I say ever so sweetly, ever taste an azalea? I pretend to bury my face in a bloom.

At least she laughs. She flops herself backward over her exercise ball and relaxes her wings.

Why don't you just ask him if he's a harpy?

Sure, she says, drop it into the conversation: "And by the way, do you happen to have wings?" What would he say but *No.* Or *Are you crazy?*

Or lie.

She drops off her ball with a bump. Okay, so he's just, you know, a little hard to read. She scrambles to her feet and heads for her room.

I take a long time folding out the couch. Every harpy emotion can be plumbed by staring into space and squawking softly for ten minutes. That Roxy should even be tempted ten years before her hundred-year cycle is up suggests something's wrong. Maybe the water isn't good for us anymore. Remind self: drink from remote streams, or just really good wines. We don't usually enjoy sex between cycles, have no real interest in it. Sometimes we get accused of being spinsters, of wearing button shoes and enjoying canasta and shuffleboard. I admit we have worn those shoes and played those games. The shoes—well, there's always the retracted claw problem, and cards are just feathers splayed out. No one ever imagines our hunched backs concealing strength rather than weakness, of us flying off the cruise ship at 3 a.m. to skim over the waves.

Let alone social work.

This isn't the first time she's been attracted to an odd duck. She must have inherited the tendency from our mother who got involved in a reverse Leda situation and actually liked the guy. Her half-human egg was too big to birth and she died in its delivery. Being at a critical point where our species may not recover, we can't afford to lose a single harpy, let alone Mom. Those few who have survived these several millennia—despite human harassment and diminishing habitat—are now practically myth, and after myth there's just the medallion, the swoosh on the side of a pair of shoes, the emblem on a family crest. Extinction.

I start worrying about Roxy, then I worry about everything else. If we can just get humans to stop abusing their children, maybe they'll stop abusing each other, and the planet.

It's my planet too.

No way am I going to tell her how ideal my leaving France was just now, indeed, how timely, how, *je ne sais pas*, critical.

Chapter 3

THE COLLINS family filed a complaint against you, says Tim. Already.

He's hunched in that leather jacket of his, a bird trait, yes, but it's a trashed look, same pair of pants worn for a week. When we're about to flower, what we usually see is a lot of dressed-to-the-nines possibilities: puffed satin sleeves, ruffs everywhere, leather capes inscribed with heroics, purple togas, embroidered waistcoats, lace up the wazoo, the weirdest hats—and such a lot of jewelry.

I raise my fingers in a peace salute. I'm a little unfamiliar with all the procedures in social services here, I say. The baby was in danger.

Of course. He clears his throat.

What will he say? He doesn't want to jinx what he's got going with Roxy. He knows we're roommates. I help myself to a red clipboard with an attached yellow highlighter from a pile on his chair that makes his office look sort of work-festive, I steal one of his pens.

He taps a finger for the pen's return. Roxy gave you quite a good recommendation, and as you may know, I'm short-handed.

I hold my tongue. Will he fire me? Will I be subject to covert condemnation? Intermittent harassment? I almost don't care. There's something about him. A whiff of—

Stewie makes an entrance. He does this whole cock-of-the-walk thing that only husky Black guys can pull off, wearing an orange and red tie-dyed hoodie so tight you can see muscle. He throws back his chest, not in the least trodden down or *Yes, sir*, and smiles at me and Tim. Who's on the Save the Children list today? I've got life jackets.

Mr. McBride, says Tim, you're ten minutes late.

I had to help a little girl cross the street, says Stewie.

He's so forthright about it, Tim almost smiles. Guess you'd better get yourself off the street then and into the van. Coco's staying here. She's doing the processing this morning.

I give Tim a big pseudo-relieved smile, as if I really did fear for my job. But instead of allowing him a chance to look too deeply into my irises which, like many animals', reveal that I've seen everything, I lower my head in a nod, and return his pen. He registers all this by frowning at the underpaid, nearly underage new social work graduate I'm pretending to be.

There's something about him.

I wolf down the suet that Roxy's only eaten half of. She's always dieting because pecans are her weakness. Talk about calories. I love a lunchroom, I tell her: the smell of tuna, soggy cheese, the raisins escaping. It sure beats the troughs of yore.

Tim, sighs Roxy. She turns her head away as if she were still a smoker, to suggest a thoughtful break.

I pop the pomegranate seeds I always pack, one at a time, as if they're an antidote to what I hear. You've got it bad. I mean, Tim's not ugly, but.

Tim, she sighs again, expelling enough air to inflate a soccer ball.

I choke on a seed so it doesn't sound as if I'm laughing. He's okay but not that okay. He's only been on the job six weeks.

I've only been in his office three. Before that, there was the hall, there was the water fountain. She pretends she's one of those eternally dipping birds.

I'm laughing for real this time.

Stewie comes around with a plate of kale and crackers. Another Black kid shot up by cops, he says, shaking his head. How does that exactly work with social services? He takes a seat beside us.

Statistically, most of our clients should be dead or in jail, I say.

He brightens up as if he didn't expect me to know. Endangered, he says. He carefully places his ball cap on the table beside his plate and roughs up his kale with his fork. She's going to be a lot of fun, he says to Roxy. He takes a bite of the kale, chews thoughtfully. I forgot to ask you yesterday—you a feminist?

Men are twelve times more likely to abuse children than women, I tell him.

His eyebrows go up. She's definitely a friend of yours.

Roxy grins. I pump out my best "friend" smile. We don't like people to know we're related, two birds with one stone and all that.

But really, he says, warming to his subject, you know what it's like to be a target? He leans back and pretends to take aim at the ceiling.

I can imagine it, yes, I say.

Violence is not an answer to anything. Social is the answer and I, for one, hear it calling. He holds a hand up to his ear: Social services! he says in a high lady voice.

Oh, Stewie, giggles Roxy, I miss you. That rotation we did together—

Too short. He swallows another mouthful. You see, Coco, I tell it like it is. He rubs my shoulder with his own. It's in the smells between us, baby, and not something we see, that really makes people stay together. Kids know this.

Love stinks is what you mean, I say.

He picks up his water glass, takes a sip, smiles as if it's an elixir. Now why would a gorgeous girl like you say a thing like that?

She's never been in love in her life, says Roxy.

Poor girl, says Stewie. Too picky.

How did you get to be a member of this club? he says. He means to make conversation but it comes out sounding like an insult.

She narrows her eyes. My mother founded it. Dear Mother, she says with an ironic sigh. Who dressed me up as a different rare bird every Halloween.

He laughs. She does have a long neck. Swan? He doesn't ask. More along the lines of a duck.

The waiter arrives and they order drinks.

The jacket you came in, she says. Leather. At the risk of a cliché, it suggests you are, at heart, a rebel.

You're a shrink?

I am a doctor, she says, of ornithology. I'm good at interpreting coats of all kinds. She flashes the green bird on her ring—emerald?—and gestures toward the cross-stitched flock on her bag.

You do birds. That's when he notices a lot more of them than sailboats in the paintings on the walls, as well as stuffed specimens in cases. And you're doing a study of what? Women in social services?

What you've sent me about her has been very useful. She opens her eyes a little wider to make her smile look less condescending.

A large clock chimes in another room. The people in the club shift with the time, some into the next room, many more moving up the stairs past them. So very sad, they nod to her, one after another, about your mother. I've got plans, she responds, but without affect, as if she'd said *I've got a tan.* As soon as the last one exits, she grimaces and starts winding up, telling him about climbing a very tall dead tree and roping herself to the trunk to take a picture of a rare tit's eggs, about standing in cold river water past her knees and waiting six hours to hear a particular mating song from a particular loon to make sure she'd found the right nest, about flying to Bhutan to haggle with a supplier about a mix of seed for lure.

I've shot clay pigeons, he says.

Listen, she says, an actual northern mockingbird was stuck in the air shaft of my *pied-à-terre* for a week. It sang all night, every night, trying to attract a mate. A series of determined, very pleasant melodies. I didn't hear it today. I inquired and the doorman had gotten it with a broom.

She sits forward so he can almost see down her blouse. Is she leaning that way deliberately?

I will need her DNA, she says. She's so intense, as if she's about to pounce.

What are you trying to prove?

She laughs. I don't want you to have any preconceived notions. She rummages in her purse at her feet and produces a vial. Here, she says.

About time. I've almost finished what you sent two weeks ago.

Three drops, no more, she warns him, handing it over. A twisted smile crosses her face, as if she's just explained how to use a condom.

Chapter 5

I SUSPECT East Berliners learned all their bullying spy-counterspy paperwork from social services everywhere. I'm collating forms with questions like: *Is your husband living with you? Who gets dinner for the children? Where do they go after school?* If they could use just numbers to track the progress of the cases, they would. Numbers can't lie, can't emote, they make the "science" in "social" more obvious. Humans like everything quantified.

I could drop all this rubbish and fly back to my cushy orphanage position in France if I could just convince Roxy that Tim's all human and she should stay away from him for her own good. It's not that I don't want to hang around—I do love her—but we lead separate lives, we're territorial.

I am almost asleep on the job when a fly starts beating its brains out against the office window. It's inside, wanting out, one of those crazed fat winter flies. It suspends itself in midair, falls a foot, recovers, and is about to do it again when I catch it. Not the stiff JetBlue wings or even the hummingbirds', all frenetic and helicopter-ish and totally not fly-like, the fly's wings lie sleek and transparent beside its eyes, as if the wings can see too. I'm not one to pull them off and examine them with tweezers, but I have seen detailed pictures online of the jagged panes that hold them together, their efficient oar shape. Such beauty.

The bug pulls itself together and takes a walk around my palm. I hold my hand steady.

Fear is the primary emotion humans engender in other creatures, not love. I scorn humans for their naivete about the wisdom of other species, their begrudging whales a language and crows the ability to count. Mine is the response of a creature who's hard to kill and who's had centuries of experience with behaviors both human and animal.

I eat the fly.

I clock out ten minutes later, take the bus home. No, I don't—I duck behind a tree to release my wings. Let the bus toddle down its route without me—I'll fly, thank you very much. Who cares? Roxy's off with Pretty Boy. I'll give her an hour. I've seen the way he watches her in the lunchroom, her ass down the hall. So cute, this whole love thing, so ghastly when you consider the possibility it might kill her.

I walk the last block, inspecting the area for a tastier flying treat, something with bulk that you could actually cook with potatoes and onions, and debate whether I should just go to the store and buy the right-sized carcass dead dead dead when there's a glint from the window of a van across the street from our place. I noticed the van earlier in the week, and it hasn't moved. Somebody's inside. The very small print across the door says *Robinson's Cell Tower Installation and Service.*

And I've got good eyes.

It's not as if I haven't been surveilled before. Lots of people have wanted my tail, as it were. Once both Roxy and I ended up caged in an Arab circus, our feathers sold for silver one by one. Back then we weren't too smart and took a lure. Roxy would fall for anything shiny. Believe me, we did not enjoy being on display every second, the handfuls of barley they thought we liked to eat, the desert cold. I had to off nearly three hundred people to escape, a big job that historians credited to a mysterious plague.

Is that somebody in the van tracking me, or is it a simple voyeur? An innocent bird-watcher?

I've flown from Nice. Here is nice but Nice—all floppy French umbrellas and drinks, a glittering curve of fabulous beach—is all good. It's survived tsunamis and corrupt mayors, not to mention Queen Vic summering with the seedy poet Robert Service of Klondike fame. It's where fire was supposed to have been invented, where Barbarossa carried off two thousand captives, then dozens of pale Englishmen beached, pirates all, to compete for loot. Long before that, Medea pleaded a particularly nasty excuse for having killed her children, insisting that her *thumos,* or whatever, forced her into it—ha!—and her thugs pursued me all the way to the Mediterranean where they established the town and put me on the flag to show they had me, one conquest as good as another. That's no booted eagle flapping over the courthouse. The wind in that region I've found very useful for long flights to North America, with an eddy to Africa that tends toward Southeast Asia. The location gives me swath.

These days Interpol has its swath too, a whole world's worth. They spend their time investigating points of contact, creating big fat databases that hopefully don't include me. They get especially unhappy about questionable deeds committed over a long period of time with no discernible motive, especially since their particular métier is tapping into border data, and especially those pesky European borders that spider everywhere.

I laugh at borders, why should they stop me? I fly right over. Interpol couldn't find me if I fell out of the sky in front of them. All they can do is outsource the nabbing, and it's hard to get good results without doing it yourself. Crime for regular cops does not pay, it's the bumblers who get these jobs. That's the number one reason I'm not too worried. The other thing is that funding for the electronic wonders that the movies show the police using so cleverly to close in on their suspects, screens large with rap sheets and faces matched in seconds, has not actually happened in real life. About all the new tech the police have at their disposal is the art of texting and low-res cop cams. Drones, named after the terrible sound they make over the houses of the hunted hour after hour, may make up for this, but

I'm not sure. There have been sightings of creatures flying around unidentified for a millennium, and the mechanical ones joining them might just make for more chaos.

What I did in Greece, and later in France and England and elsewhere, is sometimes called a suicide, or an accident, or it goes mysteriously unreported. A convertible that goes over a cliff and the couple inside land in an impossible place? Put it in the file marked Witches, Warlocks and Vampires, the weird and quickly cold cases. Could it be that my offing the French president's evil nephew from on high was an error on my part? Some might think my killings casual, but no, it took me years of watching this guy filet small children before I could come out of hiding. How was I to know his death would embarrass the president with other "findings" more financial?

I should not do what I do, but there it is, a problem. I'm tweaked a little past Superman on the rescue side. Things happen. Roxy asking for help just then was fortuitous. I didn't hang around waiting for the newspapers to report on whatever the perplexed French detectives could come up with. Or cover up. Like a lot of people in the enforcement business, they value their jobs more than justice, and often even don't believe in justice—and never in me. After some rough dealings with that evil nephew, I zipped straight across the Atlantic, appearing as a blur on the very best radar. Though sailors do glimpse me now and then with the new high-powered binoculars, they can't comprehend what they see. Albatross? Anomalies are hard on humans.

You tend to think what you see is what you've always seen. Usually, they back down and deny their claims of a flying woman.

I glance at the van again. Surveillance is a very exacting stage for me. I can't run upstairs and close the curtain, that would just confirm whoever's hunch. I have to be a bit careful. Should I dye my hair and cut it, wear sunglasses? I wish I had a fake nose, but they don't come bigger than the one I already have. Wear sunglasses? My sunglasses were how people recognized me in Nice, big frames, wild colors. Here, even Roxy might get suspicious if I start wearing those all the time. Too conspicuous.

I casually stroll close to the van, out of camera range, to jot down the license plate—not that the car is owned by the guy inside, but it would be interesting if it's Tim's.

Google says zilch on my phone. Very professional.

My sister texts to say she's on her way home with a roast chicken. Perfect! I text back. Just what I was thinking. Her next text is that Tim could be one of the nonaggressive metrosexual harpy males—it could even happen to them!

I love Roxy, her enthusiasm for humans. Like everything else genetic, such enthusiasm varies from bird to bird. She believes that if humans just try something only a wee bit different, their brains will get into a wider groove, tolerance will become habit, they won't beat their cross-dressing children or any of a million other minor human deviations. She thinks parents don't mean to abuse them, it's too much testosterone in the males and too much submission in the females—but that's changing with all the hormones in the water supply. And now that humans live longer, she thinks it's easier for them to see the damage they do to their children. There's hope, she says. Roxy explains the cumulative power of these little changes in terms of chaos theory, one flap of the butterfly and all the outcomes roll out changed. If I can just be that butterfly, she says.

Oh, Roxy—if I flee this time, I leave you at their mercy.

Chapter 6

I'M FORTY-FIVE today, Robinson says to the van's rearview mirror. "Old Guy Works on Birthday." I should be paid more for increased seniority, but the office—full of high-powered infants—says what I'm getting is scale for outsourcing. And I thought departments here were rolling in the dough.

He thinks about dough, and then lunch. Where did I put the takeout menus? he mutters, rummaging through various wadded-up papers on the dash.

Maybe this Coco is a killer, but watching her from this van day after day is killing him. It's a solo job and he's putting on the pounds sitting in the van all day. It's even getting harder to crouch down to get into the back area where he keeps the hardware, and probably a menu, and sometimes he has to get there fast to change a battery. But he's got to go back there to monitor the screens anyway. He squeezes through the little door that connects front to back and hunches his way over to the La-Z-Boy in front of the controls. He can't stand up.

Flicking on three of the four screens, he sees—nobody. The front of the apartment house, the side view, and almost to the back. It's too dark in the very back for a camera, and his preliminary review of the area was that it isn't in use. He's supposed to follow her wherever if there is reasonable cause, but otherwise, no. He just has to watch. She is so, well, tedious compared to the Kardashians a few years back. He had the best lens then, you could practically see the moles on their pudenda. On the A-list for recording their monthly grocery mag exposés, he'd decided, on a whim, that switching to crime would be more exciting. Whatever gap he'd left in the A-list was instantly filled, which led him deeper into crime.

But what does this girl do except stare out the window once in a while? Since he's set up, he's seen nothing more exciting than her feeding birds in the late afternoons. No parties. No strange men. She gets up early and goes to the office. The end. He knows you have to be patient for jobs like these, that is the whole point, you can't expect car chases all the time, but if he were a real dick, he'd go up and ask a few questions. There's probably six other surveillance teams working on god-knows-how many other women for the same thing. After all, how could this one woman be at all those locations, pushing people over cliffs? That isn't exactly organized crime. Here, there, no pattern. Women don't do contract killing, at least not in his experience. The upper body strength is rarely adequate if it comes down to hand-to-hand. He's thinking the leader of this sacrificial cult—that's what it has to be, doesn't it?—has collected quite a few frequent flyer miles. And the one where the car crashes and the passengers end up a mile away? How is that even a clue? Sloppy police work.

He jots down the date/time stamp from the screen into the log, and uses the toilet, bumping his knees into the battery box. He'll review that unwatched bit of tape later, in the dark, when he doesn't have to keep his eyes on the screen so much.

A case has really gone cold, his supervisor said yesterday, when they can only afford you.

What's my dog doing?

He checks his cell phone. The monitor shows the dog sleeping, streaks of wet kibble smeared over the floor, a pile of chewed-up paper bags, probably chicken bones somewhere too. That idiot dog walker. They never think they're being watched. With this cheap gadget, he can tell when the dog goes out, how much water is left in the bowl, when he's bored. The dog isn't so happy about hanging around the house all day, day after day, without any attention, except the walker. It's like the two of them have the same lives, both trapped inside, only the dog has it better because he gets to go out once in a while and doesn't have to watch anyone, he can sleep.

Robinson carefully drapes his jacket and vest, a costume leftover from his A-list days, on a hanger clipped to a darkened side window. The fan isn't so good anymore and the ventilation never was kick ass. In his tidying up, he finds a menu underfoot. He hasn't tried the anchovy pizza yet. Worth a call. After he puts in his order, his wife texts.

She wants the dog, she says it will protect her three kids, it will protect her and them from her new man.

His job is 24/7, she knows that. He can't run over and drop off the dog. The whole reason she took up with this Greek guy, the one who doesn't like the kids so much, was because his job was 24/7 and she was lonely. Give up the boyfriend is what he texts her.

Plus the money's too good to give up this job, he can't give it up. It's his livelihood. But he hates the idea of giving up the dog. She will really have everything then.

Let's celebrate that last bit of wisdom. His cell phone's programmed with an automatic treat-feeder and he presses the button.

The dog looks toward the machine while it loads up and then nails the treat the second it flies out.

More fun.

A couple of jobs back, he had a break and returned to his apartment for a few days. His wife was still around but mopey and the kids had forgotten he liked to sleep in, but worst of all, the dog didn't seem to know him, pretended he was some kind of intruder, barked and showed his teeth. Hopefully he won't have to fight his way in when this job is over.

He could use a nap.

Pizza is what he hears next from the delivery guy, beating on his door.

No change for a tip.

Again? says the delivery man who gives him the finger.

He gobbles a slice as soon as he opens the box. Even his mom forgot his birthday. No card, no nothing. It's like being buried early. He drags another slice out of the pie. One of the advantages of dining in the back is that you can spread out a little and relax in front of the monitors. Replacing his slice, he makes his move. Except his shoelace is caught on something. He futzes with it, head down between front and back, pizza clumping up in the tipped box.

Again—someone tapping at the window. Should he answer? He is surveillance, after all, he has to stay out of sight. On the other hand, he's supposed to keep his cover. It's always a toss-up.

Wiping himself clean with the tiniest of serviettes, he clambers back into the front and rolls down the window.

Hi, I'm Coco, I live over there, where you're watching.

She's tall, he thinks. Nicely shaped close up.

I'm your cell tower adjuster, he says, clearing his throat, holding up his pizza-smeared laptop as if in explanation. I get to fiddle with the tower angles to improve your reception.

Your white van, she says, is like a house painted purple. Surveillance budgets must be slipping. Rent a mommy van, there's a million of those around here. I know, not everyone who looks at you sees you, but really can't you be a little less conspicuous?

He swallows. She's cheeky. Here's my card, he says, handing her one of the ten identities he keeps in an envelope to match whatever he's got across the van. Nice to meet you.

Mr. Robinson?

He tips the noiresque fedora he keeps low on his forehead.

I'll improve your reception, she says. She smiles, a big beautiful wide smile that just radiates cunning, and snaps off his antenna.

Chapter 7

TIM BUYS two tickets to the film and waits for Roxy in front of the theater. What's he doing running his finger around his neck to adjust his collar, pulling his jacket straight? So what if he's applied only one drop of the eau de Reagan behind his ear and it's supposed to take three? How can anyone believe that's all that's working? He puts out a little mumbo-jumbo on his own. He pets his baldness, then rubs his face, the soft slight fuzz of the early evening.

A bird, one of the little ones, lands on his shoulder and taps at his neck before he beats it off. What is it with these birds? Must be spring. He's been noticing these wild ones more. Before, they were either up in the sky or flew off whenever you walked toward them. Big deal. But now even these shrimpy birds are getting aggressive. He paces to keep them from thinking he's some kind of lamppost.

He has to admit he's been looking forward to this date. Okay, so she's attracted to him, that's always cute. But she's not so exciting that he has a lot of competition. He's not put off by the nose, and she's blonde. He's always been partial to blondes. Okay, so his mother was a blonde. That never counts. He hasn't seen his mother in what, fifteen years? About as long ago as the last time he was in public housing. And there was a high school fling even longer ago—she was blonde too. It was the next one, the one he did marry, who started blonde and then turned into a redhead. He is still angry at her for walking out on him, taking the kid. Not the crudely angry, take-a-hammer-to-her-head kind—he is over that now—just the anger of him not walking out first when he had the chance. The boy would be what? Eleven, or ten? His birthday's coming up soon. He wasn't the world's best father, but now that he has worked at this child services agency, he knows he wasn't the worst.

He scrapes mud off his shoes against the grass and the stink of wet dirt wafts up to him. He went walking in the nearby park to pretend that he liked mucking around in nature, in case Roxy arrived early and saw him. Nature lovers make good lovers is what he'd planned to tell her, or something like that, maybe something a little less direct.

If it isn't two coworkers from the office picking up tickets. They're from another corridor but he knows them well enough to exchange nods. Don't want them thinking he's interested in somebody from work. Very compromising. He looks off into the sunset after the nod thing so they don't ask who he's waiting for. He hopes she gets here after they're seated.

They go off to the car crash film anyway.

Roxy shows about a minute before the previews start, coat flapping, hair wild. She gives him a big smile. I had to lose Coco, she says, stroking her hairdo down. She said she's had the hots for this movie too. I said that's why they invented streaming.

Yeah, get a life, he says, handing over her ticket.

Coco's doing her best. It's not easy if you've been buried in the boondocks for literally ages.

I feel for her, he says, offering her cold popcorn.

He tries to watch the show instead of Roxy. It's hard, he's never sat so close to her before, or at least not for so long. Maybe she's putting out some perfume of her own. She picks at the popcorn, stretches, and he sees breasts in alluring outline. He works his arm around her and strokes her shoulder. She turns her black olive-pit eyes on him until he withdraws his arm. Sorry, he says.

He goes back to movie watching. Maybe he can pick up some tips about acting.

Afterward, she seems impatient, not stunned the way he always is after all that on-screen action. What about a walk along the water?

We could drive, he says. I've got my car just a block away.

A walk is romantic, she says, it's healthy.

Those eyes of hers.

Okay, he says, lengthening the word out so she can tell he's still hesitant—it's not his style, letting a woman take the lead—but he goes walking with her anyway, up one street and down another, all the way to where you can see the water, talking about nothing, just talking. On the bridge, she stops and turns to him and asks: Do you think you're in love with me?

I don't know, he says, taken aback. He knows enough to stop walking. It's kind of early.

She's about a foot away and folds her arms across her chest. All over Europe, people buy locks and put them on bridges, a kind of pledge of love. You see them everywhere.

I've never been to Europe. I've eaten snails though.

Maybe you are an idiot, she says. She puts her arms on his shoulders. Could you love me?

He pulls his jacket around his middle, wedging her away. Yeah, he says. That's the problem.

I agree. She steps even closer, sniffing his ear. I won't tell anybody. She pulls him to her, grips him tight, wraps her arms around him. He nuzzles her, he plucks a feather from the back of her sweater. Of course it could have fallen from a tree but—

They kiss. Finally. She's played so hard to get before now, she's like somebody's grandma.

She paws him and kisses him harder, she pulls up his shirt in back and strokes his skin—sexy!—then she scratches him deep and hard across his back.

He wrenches away. Cut it out, he yelps. What are you doing?

Love is a dangerous thing, she says, curling her fingers into her fist. That was the point of the movie, not the chase scenes.

He can't believe she hurt him—he can't remember a thing about the movie—is he actually bleeding? He tucks his shirt in.

If he weren't being paid to do this.

She's just standing there, her head cocked, her lipstick smeared.

Look, we could fly to Europe when my vacation time comes up, it's not that expensive, he says. I'll get a lock.

Yeah, she says, flying's the way to go. She walks back fast, walks faster, even a few steps ahead of him. He has to trot alongside all the way back to the car.

What should he have said?

Chapter 8

IMAGINE THE pressure of air all around, gravity pulling from below, the velocity you need to ignore it. I relax into the air eventually, I lean into the current, not flapping, not diving, the upside of the earth palm-open under me. I forget, every time, the thrill and beauty of soaring. I must always forget or I'd never spend ten minutes on earth, stuck upright on such heavy feet, plodding forward. Omniscient, the view—and the responsibility of seeing so much dissipates when everything below appears so small. It's a relief not to worry about humans for a while, the way they tend not to give an ant a leg up, but just watch with amusement while the tiny brown bits swirl down the sink.

Of course I actually kill people.

Oomph! Roxy hits me hard in midair. Tim's a harpy, she screeches.

The DNA?

His genes are definitely screwed up.

Did the lab know why? I squawk, pumping the air.

They weren't looking for a harpy. She swoops and returns with a big smile across her face. Anyway, he does like birds.

I know. At least one.

We fight and we tumble as if we were still teenagers. I grip her feathers with my teeth, we plummet. One of us has to bail quick, there's no special dispensation from gravity for harpies. Our wings pound.

Chapter 9

SATURDAYS ROXY likes to watch over children who aren't in social services—yet. She says she's lost touch with kids in her current job with all the paperwork. For some reason— maybe the animals all caged up—zoos attract bad parents, according to her. She has her theories and says the very worst cases can't take time off from being bad to go to the zoo, they're too busy with abuse, but the next worst parents like to get out of the house. She's gotten a lot of this from a class she took on parenting at the local college. Not that she's ever raised a human, or mostly human, like I have.

I've always avoided zoos. There's so much bird in me, I feel sorry for the animals. Surely some of them are cross-beings like us, just stuck with green skin or retractable teeth and no way to tell us. But Roxy's even talked me into driving there. I roll down my window for air. She knows how much I love the feeling of the wind and drizzle on my face and me behind the controls—it's a lot like flying.

Who cares about my hair? My sister accuses me of being a tomboy, so much do I not care.

A small tapir herd on the other side of the zoo fence is eating eating eating like the pigs they resemble. Content. Seemingly. At least nothing like the pacing, roaring carnivores at the other end of the road. After parking the car tapir-side, I pick a brochure off the pavement and flash my sister the cute pictures. Says right here animals always take good care of their young, if their habitat is right.

Propaganda, she says. The usual grass-is-greener.

It used to be me making those grand statements about animals and humans. You're finally getting the picture.

She laughs but she doesn't disagree. It took her a lot longer to see how much humans are more like other animals than like us.

We head for the gorilla enclosure. Another of my sister's ideas: chest-beating inspires humans to beat on each other, releases macho pheromones, thus aggression, and aggression is catching. I nod toward the biggest gorilla. He probably knows what we are. Animals are better than humans at detecting real aberration. This one immediately starts maneuvering on his knuckles toward me.

Two little girls, about five, run screaming into the presentation area, one chasing the other. Perfect. I hover. My sister is bending over a three- or four-year-old blind boy in a stroller who has a broken arm, listening to him trumpet like an elephant. His parents are on their cell phones, their backs turned. Before the two little girls realize that they're lost and start crying, the blind boy shrieks at my sister: *Bird, bird,* so loud everyone hears him.

Sensitive child. But he's blind and a kid, so who's going to believe him?

Now, now, my sister says to the boy.

Bird! The boy is so insistent, he bangs his cast on the railing.

His mother puts down the phone she's so fascinated by and thrusts her head toward my sister. He's handicapped— can't you see? Leave him alone.

When the boy turns toward me, I see the outline of an old burn on his cheek.

We were just chatting, says my sister.

A mother holding a dawdling toddler pushes through the door and the lost girls run to her. Good. Just in time. I turn to confront the woman with the phone. Who blinded the boy? I hiss. And how could a child his age break a bone?

Her husband looks up from his cell.

You're crazy, says the woman in a whisper. She leans down to the boy, but he holds his cast up to his face as if to ward off her touch.

Conflict sets off the gorillas, who are uneasy anyway, ever since I nodded to the big one, now beating his chest. Roxy's right, nothing brings in people like chest-beating. They show up from all over, through doors and corridors, and press close to get a better look. In the disorder, the mother jerks the blind boy's stroller past the crowd, while the father, on the phone again, holds the door open to the next exhibit, but not long enough, and it clips the stroller wheel.

I saw a little of that, says Tim, who shows up out of nowhere and takes my sister's hand. Kind of vigilante, wouldn't you say?

I keep my hissing to myself. Delighted to see you, I say. You texted him?

My sister admits nothing. After a pause so long it seems profound, my sister says to Tim, Hi. She's suddenly meek, her shoulders bow, making her look tiny, although she's actually taller than he is, then she smiles and dimples appear, her cheeks go pink, her eyes shine. In short, she turns attractive.

Are you two always going to be together? asks Tim, steering us out the door opposite the blind boy's exit. Very devoted. Maybe there's something you want to tell me, he says to my sister. Are you two—you know—

She laughs and tosses her head as if I were no one at all, much less a lover.

Don't you have a Maserati to buff or something? I say. What are you doing here anyway?

I love zoos. He gives me teeth with that smile of his; they say *Give it a rest*.

My sister admires him as he pushes through the exit, the kind of *Ooh* I've seen that can really derail the brains of anything female.

We follow him onto the walkway. He puts his arm around her, and she sniffs his neck. He's always generous with the cologne, even I can smell it. Since it's the weekend, he's not barefaced but whiskery with the stubble men leave to suggest too much testosterone. It gives off a scaly shine in some lights when he turns his bald head slowly. Which he's doing now, looking for a signpost.

The aviary. I knew it.

I'm a big fan, he says. I'll show you my favorites.

I tell him we never visit the aviary. It's too depressing: the confined space, the competing species, old molting everywhere and the sad bird calls, the saddest in the world.

My sister says she's curious.

Curious, please.

We're standing beside the albino peacock that screams as soon as it sees us and screams even louder when Tim pushes bird seed through the screen. They're so beautiful, he says.

So are the beetles in the next exhibit, I say, hungry for the seed. My sister's watching him hypnotize the peacock, waving the seed between his fingers back and forth, getting hypnotized herself.

Many people find birds frightening, I say. It's their flapping wings, some ancient fear of getting their hair tangled in the talons, or the beaks pecking out their eyes. Or maybe it's just their droppings coming down out of nowhere. Or Hitchcock. Are you a birder?

My sister drags her eyes away from Tim's swaying fingers, up to his face. So much hope.

He presses the last seed through the screen and the peacock snaps it down. When I was in high school, an old woman handed me a paper bag on my way home and walked off. Inside was a baby robin. I tried to keep it alive by wrapping it in a towel and parking it next to a lightbulb. The robin chirped like mad. I thought I'd saved it, but after an hour it went quiet. It wasn't asleep—the light bulb had cooked it. The robin was making noise because it was dying.

Guilt, you like birds because you're guilty, I say. That's probably why you're in social services too. What exactly did you do to humanity?

Let's just enjoy ourselves, says my sister.

Tim growls as if he's just been let out of his own cage. My sister thinks that's funny.

We wander the rest of the aviary. The birds go berserk as we approach, too loud for any conversation, as usual with unfamiliar birds. My sister can't keep her hands off him after his baby bird speech, trying to stroke his back every time he turns it, to verify his harpiness.

What do you think? I say when we go off to the Ladies'.

He's so attractive. She gets that look I'm beginning to fear.

There are two kinds of people who go into social service: those who love kids and those who like authority over kids.

I think you're jealous, she says. In fact, he said he worked in the police force before this. He decided he wasn't doing much good and wanted to fix things with people, not put them away.

I think Tim has experience with the police, yes, I say.

Roxy laughs. Prison was always a good roost for you.

A low blow. Just because she prefers to run away instead of fight when there's trouble. My inability to walk off makes me a good person to call if you're thinking of doing something stupid, but you have to be okay with applauding the result. He's weird, that's all, I say without conviction. You like weird.

She doesn't deny that. She once spent months soaring over the Amazon to get close to a branch of a very big eagle family to study their nests. Or so she said. The he-bird was nearly her size. She could've gone to Greece or the Caribbean or almost anywhere else where nest building is even more stagey but no, she said she wanted to build something really complicated, the logic being she would attract a better male harpy.

Tim appears to be bored out of his skull by the time we rejoin him. Granted, he was stationed next to the sloths where there's only a video replay of the last time one of them moved three weeks ago. Where next? he says with enthusiasm meant only for my sister.

We're happy enough to call it quits since we can't intervene full-out while Tim's along. On our way to the exit, my sister picks up a toddler who has tripped while the mother was shouting at him, I shove a bag of popcorn into the hands of a kid with a black eye. Normally we'd follow that blind boy we met in the gorilla enclosure but we really can't now, not with Tim here. At the gate, he takes my sister's hand and admires her nails—she's just had them done—then kisses her palm, about the sexiest thing ever, judging from her expression, and says he has to go pick up his dry cleaning.

We walk to the other end of parking. He's toying with you, I say. That baby bird story? It was on YouTube last week, the bird singing then suddenly stopping, the weeping kid afterward.

My sister is holding her palm out in front of her as if she'll never use her hand again. He moved his file drawer closer to mine last week, she mews. He said he liked the way I held my head.

You've got a beak the size of an eagle's, I say.

It's inherited, she says. Look in the mirror. It's attractive.

I have trouble finding the car. Shouldn't Tapir come before Tiger? We march past one row after another while I enumerate more reasons why Tim shouldn't be interested. Your back hunches when you're really eager, I tell her, you stick your scrawny neck out when you get excited. I look down another row. You never did get the orthodontia you were supposed to, insects stick to your teeth, and your legs are like twigs.

So?

I use the car honker on my keychain. Do we hear anything back? Nothing. My sister makes the same sound with her lips and *Voila!* the car returns her call.

No wonder nobody ever comes on to you, I laugh. With a voice like that.

We're headed for the exit when I see a certain white van parked beside the gate. When we pull parallel to it, I stick my hand out the window and make a wild gesture toward the sky.

It always works. The lens tips up, and I goose the car into traffic.

Chapter 10

ROBINSON BELCHES. Two weeks already. He fights his way through the old pizza boxes to the front seat. He wants to sit in front for a while but he should stay at the monitor because yesterday something actually happened: he caught the suspect killing a bird on the windowsill with her bare hands and then she ate it raw—and her roommate stood by and picked her teeth. Very dainty.

He sinks behind the wheel.

The sight scared him at first. It wasn't a celebrity noshing celery. At least the blonde one's a real looker. He wishes she were the one he had to keep tabs on. He does a little research on her because well, he has time, and since the turnover at that kind of social work job must be fierce, he's probably the only one who knows how long she's been at it—at least twenty years. Must be the hair that makes her look so young, or that expensive cream his wife keeps harping on that she says she needs so desperately.

After they feast on this bird, he can't make anything out

on the video until the window's empty and they've gone. A big blur. But it's not like he jiggled the camera.

He watches. There's something about seeing things with your own eyes.

Chapter 11

ROXY STARES at her spoon. Your *Ignore him* policy is driving me crazy.

It's a test of love.

You're supposed to only test for harpiness.

Ding.

Roxy accepts her bowl of chicken soup and blows on a spoonful.

I heat my own bowl in the microwave. Didn't you ask him if he loved you right after you saw that cheesy movie together? Who is pushing the envelope here?

You've been spying on me.

Privacy is a concept developed by people who have some reason to hide. I'm protecting you. I add a little sriracha to my soup. I like it hot.

Right, she says. She's so annoyed she makes a disgusted cluck and slurps at her bowl.

The Collins' hearing on the complaint about me is coming up soon. I'd forgotten all about it.

You didn't do anything else to them, did you?

I didn't need to. When Stewie went there yesterday to get their signatures on some documents, the drinkers had a science experiment set up in the bathroom, and it wasn't just the vinegar and baking soda kind.

They must be really out of it if he can just go in and see their stuff.

I fish for a noodle stuck to the inside of my bowl. They're accusing me of aggravating the situation. No specifics. Do you think Tim even likes me? Scratch that—do you think he will defend me? Does he even like children?

He loves children. She puts down her bowl as if that's end-of-discussion.

I don't see him rushing out to help them on the playground.

Lay off. You're just paranoid.

That's what I'm here for. If I get implicated in this Collins case, he'll have a lot more time with you. I set my bowl in the sink and collect hers. Does Tim have a favorite cologne?

Are you thinking of getting him a gift?

Come on. I think he's got our number and has concocted something that blinds us to his real motives.

Love? she asks.

Has he given you any real indication of that?

Now she really looks annoyed. Not really, she admits.

I start unloading the dishwasher, I squint at a glass to decide if it's been washed or not.

You know, she says, turning toward me, I miss him when I'm here with you, I miss him all the time. I actually want to live with him, make love to him. I don't want to wait another practically ten years to do it.

I keep putting things away. She slams a few plates out of the dishwasher herself as if it helps her think.

It's a drag that one of us is wired so much closer to humans, I say into her silence. At least with regard to reasoning.

The dishwasher is officially empty.

You should've been a nun, she says, flopping to the couch. Maybe it's his looks I like. Maybe it's just him. The way he comes into the room. His bald head. Not seeing him is like an eternity to me.

All right, all right. I face her before she can wall me off with her computer. What you're saying is the high possibility of laying and going out because of a human, this appeals to you. The whole drama. Think of this in reverse. Would a human ever choose to mate with a harpy if she knew she would die? Women are always thinking they'll never get knocked up, it won't happen to them. Humans just lose it when it comes to sex. But you're a harpy. You can be rational.

She looks at her screen. I'm in love and you're not. And maybe it will work out. Maybe he's a harpy too and there won't be any problem. Besides, who else would be attracted to me? She looks up. Just saying.

The usual female insecurity. She's had a long time

between compliments and they seem to be getting more important to her these days. Very important.

I pretend to work, I shuffle papers, I open my own computer. We're at the end of an argument where I can't do any good. I flap, that's about it. Papers—and a few feathers—fall to the floor around me.

I think we're both molting, I say.

You don't make me that nervous.

What is it then? I lean over and pick up one of the feathers—hers? mine?—and try to tickle her.

She avoids my eyes.

You're getting so human you think I'm into romance too? Roxy thinks Coco wants Tim too?

Roxy doesn't really laugh, and the feather drifts off my finger.

I'm peeking through the curtain, pecking at a pear, thinking about the eyedrops the guy must have to use to sit there all day doing nothing nothing nothing maybe hallucinating, hopefully hallucinating, and having leg cramps sitting so long, and I'm wondering what is Robinson waiting for? And how can I really make a difference with kids if he's as tight as a tick on me all the time? All I really know is that I have to try harder to go by the rules because if he apprehends me, that will make protecting Roxy impossible, not to mention my freedom.

I toss the pear core into recycling. I must be evolving like everyone else—I just don't like the seeds anymore. Out the window, a woman's crossing the street, bent over the head of a small boy in too-big shorts. He's skipping along the asphalt, yet she keeps up, follows his bouncing as he chatters away. He laughs after she says something to him, but then stumbles. Are his shoes too big? She hoists him to her hip and nuzzles the top of his head and they clear the curb.

It's hard to hire someone to love like that, she has to be his mother. At the far corner, in deep shade, a man whistles and steps out, the boy kicks to be set down, and both the woman and the boy run toward him. Up, up—the boy is swept into the man's arms and pressed to his chest, then kissed on both cheeks. So passionate. An absent father? Joint custody? Will the woman walk away and leave them? No, he puts his arm around her waist and kisses her too, a kiss long enough that the boy, now perched on the man's shoulders, pounds on his skull. The two adults separate, laugh, kiss the boy all over again.

Seriously, I shout to my sister fussing in the kitchen, some of them have it together. Did you see that? Do you think Tim could be a father?

I'd have to find out, wouldn't I? Roxy says, not without sarcasm.

Love, love, love. Later that day at work, I have to rethink it again. The attendees at my first foster parent meeting turn out to be mothers without any other way to support themselves, professional mothers with professional attitudes. I am reminded of wet nurses, how callous some of them were in the eighteenth century, letting babies die of starvation when they weren't getting paid. Here it's *Don't give me the AIDS baby; I don't want special needs because I've got needs of my own.* One young couple stumbles in with concern in their eyes, they want to adopt but slowly, foster care first, to see if parenthood is for them. Rent to buy. But what about the kid? What if it's good for him but not them? Who wants to be in Returns?

My husband is sorry he can't be here, says the woman next to me. He had such a wonderful time when Olive came home for her birthday. All twelve of the others we had showed up to celebrate.

Olive was a real handful, answers the woman across the table. You were something for her. Crack babies I hear cry 24/7 six months straight. She gone into mechanics?

And two more kids found jobs at the post office, says the mother. Barry's still the smallest guy in high school on account of the fetal syndrome, but the youngest thinks she's going to be an astronaut. More likely an accountant, I think, she is so good with her numbers.

I ponder this exchange. The old woman in a shoe—she didn't know what to do. This one did. Mom's half-human baby, the one I had to raise after she died, cried pretty hard once in a while—but not six months straight. I couldn't have managed that.

Chapter 12

TIM SIPS a scotch at the Club with Reagan. She isn't as formally dressed this time, she's in a skirt but without the pearls. He's wearing the tux that she sent him so he doesn't have to go through all that embarrassing borrowing. She hadn't imagined a professional without one, that's how much she knows about the rest of the world. Anyway, she could have saved the dough and met him on a street corner for all he cares. He's not really complaining, he likes the new get-up, makes him feel very Bondsy. It's the movie uniform for his line of work, although they're not supposed to exchange anything work-related in the way of paper at the Club in sight of the waiter, who then must ask that they put away whatever looks like work. Club rules, she tells him. Tim's not happy without paper for confirmation and produces a sheet from inside his coat anyway that she glances at. My bill to date, he says.

I'll PayPal you when I get home—hey, Fred, she says

to one of the workmen going by with a stuffed bird in his arms, I've changed my mind. Take that to the basement.

Clutching the bird tighter, Fred nods and turns down another corridor.

She puts the bill under her scotch to absorb the condensation.

Two more workmen emerge from the back, lugging a flock of albatross.

Why are we meeting here again? he asks. Somebody will notice for sure.

She settles back into her uncomfortable chair. This is one of the last places without surveillance. The only signal they catch is if you're in a hurry. That would seem suspicious. Put it in the basement with the bookcases, she tells the two men. Since my mother's death, we're going in a new direction, she says.

He nods, as if *of course.*

She drains her glass, showing her long white throat down to her cleavage. They all think you're my new lover.

I'm flattered, he says. But blackmail was his first thought, how easy it would be. Surely this woman has a rich husband. Or—maybe not. She doesn't seem like mating material. His next thought is Roxy, how he wouldn't want her to know about his blackmailing if they really got involved.

An affair will definitely put them off, he says with emphasis on *definitely.*

Wit will get you only so far. She looks over her shoulder at the arrival of the next set of workmen. I need more extensive notes for my research. And—something else. You'll see in my new briefing.

He nods. The more notes he sends her, the more she knows about Roxy, but the longer he does this courtship thing, the more he wants it to last. Roxy's been ignoring him lately and that just makes him more interested. One of the workmen bumps the corner of a fireplace painting and they both watch as he straightens so very carefully. Is there a safe behind that one?

Safes are for people with inadequate means, she says. The members here own banks. They are so old-money that two centuries ago their forebears would cut off the ear of anybody poaching one of their pigeons. I remember your story about shooting those made of clay. She eyes him as if he's just shown up, then gestures with her glass. I really like the painting behind you. It's allegorical. See the bird in the far corner?

He cranes around. The yellow one?

Goldfinches were supposed to have plucked the thorns out of Christ's head. They also appear in Bosch's work, but giant, the size of the humans.

He blusters as if he knew this already but he's not convincing and he ends up nodding, he ends up looking as if he's learning something. Your previous briefing was short with regard to her, he says. Very hypothetical.

Allegories are what made me think I could find a specimen, she says. They are usually based on some fact, like the flood in the fossil record or fables about dragons in

England that turned out to be dinosaurs. I mean, that's the way science works—an intuition, then theory, and with luck, its physical embodiment.

You also said, he says, no one has ever survived in a battle to catch one of them.

The ancient texts are not conclusive. She's only a bird, after all. With a toss of her head, Reagan asks for the results of his study.

He buries his hand in his breast pocket and produces a small plastic container.

She opens it. Her breath ruffles the feather. The last one someone brought me from a bird stakeout was from a coat lining, she tells him, very carefully replacing it back in the container. You find her pretty? A pretty bird? Her voice imitates a parrot perfectly.

Funny.

He wants to say, Isn't what Roxy's doing good for the world? Why not just let her be? But empathy is not so useful in this line of work. She's pretty, he says.

The question is, at least in terms of art, should a priceless painting decorate the wall of someone uneducated about its achievement? We'll get this tested to confirm her pricelessness. Even though I'm inclined to believe the result will be positive, what I want you to do next is a little more intimate. I want you to confirm physically what I've outlined in my briefing.

He beckons the waiter for a final free drink.

You don't have to photograph her in the nude. I will take verbal affirmation. One step at a time.

He does not return her intense, impersonal smile. Social services is very taxing, he says. I remember how it was when I was in the system.

She waves her hand. In encouragement?

I get confused, he says, and stiffens in his chair. Caught up in it, I was once so against all the bureaucracy, and now I have to help make it happen.

Help? she says, as if the idea is new. Just remember, you're there to help me. She opens her purse—the club does allow women to bring their purses with them, just not a brief-case—and tucks the container with the feather inside. I'm actually in a hurry, she says. I have a presentation to make at the Club's annual meeting in June. I need it to be spectacular.

She gestures toward the painting where the sun is coming up behind the birds, lighting their feathers, making them glow gold, suggesting that their beauty's worth far more than just the beholder's gaze. But, she says, that depends on what you produce.

Chapter 13

COCO, SAYS Tim, half of him already in my cubicle, we need help with the pickups and drop-offs today. Want another chance?

It was only a matter of time. He's definitely understaffed. Why else would it be so easy to get the job? Or did he capitulate because with me gone, it's easier to make his moves on Roxy? Should I insist I stay and protect Roxy, or protect children?

I locate my clipboard. I have to get out of the office.

We need to pick up a truant, says Stewie, pulling his sweatshirt over his head. We'll probably have to drag him out of the house on his heels, stoned or drunk. Fun.

Why so late? I'm looking for my scarf. School will be practically over by the time we bring him in.

We have to wait until it's clear he actually is a truant. It's a service we do for the county when the agency's low on revenue, he says. He dangles the van's keys. Or maybe you don't want to come. He's real big for twelve.

I flex a bicep. I've got super powers, I say.
Stewie thinks I'm hilarious.

I too was once a truant. During that critical period when I wasn't fully fledged and had to keep fluttering back to the nest for lessons from my mother on human etiquette and posture and pronunciation and landing, I skipped out for quite a bit of it. I was a wild child, probably why I ended up caring for my mother at the end, looking for forgiveness. She was one of the first harpies to show a fascination with humans, the dominant yet somewhat irrational species. She was also the first to believe her chicks would make it in the human world and trained us to blend in. We were supposed to practice walking and mimicking whatever human languages on the sly all those centuries, in the dark of a hedgerow or on the mudflats, or while they ducked into some cave to get high. She had terrible posture problems when she first dropped out of the lowest branches, and her accent? For a long time, all she could do was caw. Although our beaks have shrunken over time, we still have trouble finding decent shoes, and up to the seventeenth century, we often went around veiled—habits, hijabs, whatever—hiding as much as we could. But of course, hiding difference doesn't improve tolerance.

Being the bird that I am, back then I didn't want to know how to ingratiate myself, I didn't want to pass. On my own so early, I hobbled around insisting that people accept me for what I was. Instinct was all that compelled me to collect dried dung to make fires to keep kids warm and tell fortunes to improve parental expectations. People thought I was a gypsy with my raven hair and nose-of-a-size but there was little else I knew how to do at the time. Was anybody going to teach me anything? No. A definite truant.

The truant's apartment is three flights up. I knock and the parent is quick, he's at the door as if he's standing behind it. So glad you're here, he says, and he looks it.

Parents are not usually glad. They should be but so much pressure comes to bear on them, they can't see help when it's in front of them. I want to ask Stewie what the deal is here but when I glance back at the van, he's staring into the file. I, on the other hand, can't hold myself back. I step right in, expecting something to fall on my head or beat at my legs. This parent's older, gray-haired, jeans-clad, T-shirted, and his arm is bleeding where he says the kid has bitten him. Kid-cries come from the next room.

I find the boy barefoot, tied to a chair that's tied to a door. He stops howling when he sees me and half smiles. He's rangy in the lip-gnawing, nail-bitten way of the too-fast growth of that age.

Tying him up isn't such a good idea, I say to the parent as I bend down to undo all the knots.

He says it's the only way he could keep him from running until we got there. I didn't want to use these, he says, and raises a gnarled set of fists. Excuse me, he says, grabbing his keys. I have to get to work, and he runs out the door. Do what you can.

Get lost, screams the kid after his dad. Then, as soon as I get his hand free, he slaps me. I catch and grip that hand hard. Let me go, he shouts, you can't touch me, it's the rules.

Your rules, I say. We'll call this endangerment. When it looks as if I've almost got his second hand loose, I grab him by both wrists. By then Stewie's walking in.

The pages were out of order, he says, and checks off something on his clipboard. This is Mr. Chris Brannon.

Chris lunges, tries to bite Stewie.

I twist his arms behind his back, I pull him close.

Coco's a real strong lady, says Stewie, smiling.

What's the real problem here? I ask.

I don't want to go to school, he says. Don't make me.

I nod into the top of his head. He's shaking, really wound up.

What's wrong with school? I ask. Your friends are there.

He's not talking.

Stewie hates truants. He was saying on the way over that he sat through all those school years, he endured it and so can everybody else. Teachers don't mean any harm, he says to the kid. And you might learn a little, especially about how to get along. It's just like, what, six hours a day, he says, not counting lunch?

He probably doesn't count lunch, do you? I ask. Do you?

Chris says nothing.

Other kids giving you trouble? asks Stewie. Big bad gangs?

The kid pushes so hard against my hidden talons, I decide to release him. He windmills away, takes a corner, and rubs his arms.

It's too late for third period, says Stewie. We'll drop you at the principal's office and then you're going into detention for the rest of the day.

The kid kicks at him.

You know, says Stewie, I could have been the head of a big corporation a couple of times already but I chose this, I chose you.

That was a big mistake, says the boy.

They glare at each other.

Just get along, says Stewie. The rest doesn't matter.

The mother's not listed here, I say, glancing at the form. Where is she?

I was wondering the same thing, says Stewie. Divorced?

Chris shakes his head No, then he takes two steps toward me and grabs a skateboard tilted up in the corner beside the fridge.

Nice board, Stewie says, wrestling it away. He's actually smart, he says to me. It's in the report.

The kid gets a smart look on him. Give that back. I have to find my shoes, he says. And the books.

You still have books you carry around? I'm impressed, says Stewie. And maybe homework?

The kid opens the door he was tied to. Inside is a closet-sized room with clothes mostly strewn on the floor, and a backpack. I have to change, he says. This shirt has a hole. He makes one with a jerk to the sleeve, and holds out his hand for the skateboard.

Two beats and Stewie gives in, hands him the board. The kid slams the door in our faces.

I retreat a few steps, look back at Stewie who says, Your call.

We hear things being tossed, we hear what might be books being stacked, then it gets awfully quiet, except for some banging. Maybe he's trying to remember where he put his homework? Chris? I shout, knocking on the door, then Stewie pushes it open.

The boy and the skateboard are gone. I hadn't noticed the locks around the air conditioner but it's the window above them that's tipped open just enough to slip through. He's jerry-rigged a bungee-corded book to hit the wall now and then as if he were still in there, giving him time to get down the fire escape.

Don't look so sad, says Stewie. You'll get another chance, I'll bet we'll see plenty more of him.

I don't say anything until we're back at the car, then I can't resist: Won't Tim be furious for not bringing him in?

Stewie is maneuvering slowly out of the drive as if he's

afraid he'll run over the missing boy. The kid'll be home as soon as we leave, he says. It's not like he's really running away. And Tim? He hasn't been on the job long enough to terminate anybody, and I'm not sure he will be.

Why's that?

Chris's apartment complex disappears behind us, its attempt at a fence, the two half bushes up against it that need water. He smells, Stewie says.

Perfect character analysis, I say to him, laughing.

Say, you know anything about the white van that's always coming up behind us? says Stewie.

I check the rearview mirror. My ex.

He's really taking an interest.

Not to worry, I've got it all under control.

Women, says Stewie, and swings his dreads like *No way*.

Chapter 14

TIM SEES Coco down the hall by the lockers, talking to somebody. The hall is narrow. He's going to have to pass by pretty close. What the hell, she can't avoid him forever.

Okay, Oxy's with her.

They both startle when they see him.

Talking about me? He leans his arm against the locker to look cool.

Do I look that guilty? says Coco.

He's helpless to prevent a grin from crossing his face, the direct result of being so close to Roxy. She's not even smiling, she's just standing there with clouds passing through her head. Or else her brain's going a thousand miles a minute. How about a picnic on the island? she says out of nowhere, as if she's been planning this for a week.

Sure, he says, the word whipping out of him a little too fast.

We have a lot of work to do, says Coco. You were going to throw out stuff when you got home.

You can come too, says Roxy. He won't be so forward that way.

He laughs *ha-ha*. I'll bring the picnic blanket.

After a two-second standoff between Coco and Tim, Roxy pokes her. And I'll pick up the snacks, she says. It'll be fun.

Tim's carrying a bag from the liquor store when they meet up. He knew wine would make a better impression with Roxy than the six-pack he really wanted. He takes her bag of this and that—celery, unbelievable—and Coco's, and can't think of another thing to say, although he feels very cocky with two of them on the line, even if it was Roxy's idea.

Water's the best spot for romance, says Coco, turning to him at the railing while the ferry pulls out. He doesn't trust her, the way she bats her eyelashes so sarcastically behind those weird sunglasses of hers, but what can he do? Roxy giggles but keeps her eyes on the scenery. Or at least pretends to. The sun won't be setting for at least another hour, plenty of time to check her out.

The island is pretty empty, a lot of cliffs, wind, all that water caught between rocks. He's never been here before but he's heard about it. Probably really nice in a couple of months when it gets warmer. The breeze out here isn't from the city; it's fresh.

This place is protected half the year, he says, reading from the signpost at the dock.

Protected from what? asks Coco, picking up some trash.

Roxy laughs. Us. There's some rare bird on the beach and it's their laying season soon.

They watch the rare bird dive and swoop and disappear into the water. It gets the girls excited, they run all over the place, tossing rocks or sticks at the waves, both of them climbing the stumpy tree at the end of the point, backs to each other, the wind tearing at their clothes, just staring at the water. With their hair flying around their faces, they could be sisters, they look so much alike—except for the blonde versus black. By the time he picks his way over the rocks, Coco is pointing to a couple of the rare birds. Look how the male flaps his wings over the Mrs., she shouts to him over the wind, the blank look on the female.

It's all about pheromones, says Roxy, pushing a blonde strand out of her eyes. All the data inside them that needs expressing.

Data, he says, putting his arm around her, pulling her to him. She doesn't resist.

They drag pieces of driftwood together to sit on. Roxy laughs when she sees there's still a price tag on the blanket he puts down. He laughs too, playing up the courtship angle, the scheming clumsy bachelor. All the time he's thinking about how to bag Roxy.

Okay, that's not what he's thinking the whole time.

They share the feast they've brought but, except for a bag of nuts and the celery, they hardly eat anything, *like birds*, he thinks, a little drunk, and he is going to have to haul most of it back. He himself will eat anything that comes in cellophane. He chews down a piece of the celery, tough as a log, for looks. Jesus, he should just nab her and get this over with. All he has to do is strip her in a dark corner to check for birdiness. Easy. Right now, though, he's liking this polite little family they make, even Coco isn't being so hard on him. Cut, cut, he thinks to himself, to the next scene where he's driving a million-times-better car.

He follows Roxy to the restroom with the empties. She ducks inside. He hoists the recycling to the container and crash! that's the end of the bottles. Then she's looming over him, so tall he's all of a sudden afraid, a jerk-back fear like the kind you have seeing a snake you don't expect. She bends her neck down fast, her face gets so close to his that he has to kiss her and he does and he feels it again, the passion drawing up from his groin into his brain where it's soft, he kisses her seriously. Is this where the clothing comes off? I shouldn't like you so much, he says when they part.

Afraid you'll lose your job?

My job, yeah, he says, stroking her hair. That's it.

She catches his hand and kisses his fingers. Let me tell you about myself, she whispers into them.

The ferry bellows its exit from the other side of the island.

Don't.

Her eyes go wide.

I mean, he says, let's keep the mystery going.

Yes, she says slowly, why didn't I think of that?

Coco comes around just then with a big *Ahem,* and they untangle themselves.

Lost? asks Roxy.

Coco stuffs the beach trash into the bin and walks off.

To placate her, he gives Coco a kid's fishing rod he found in the garage he's renting. It comes together pretty fast, and for bait she agrees that the leftover snack doodles and a few gummy worms will be perfect. Roxy laughs at Coco trying to fix the lure and then, reeling and cursing, Coco threatens to make her try. In the meantime, he untangles a net he brought in another bag, thinking he'll show his prowess by flinging it into the ocean and catching fish by the bushel.

He swings the net over his head and casts it into the water. It lands right on top of Roxy. Caught you! he yells as if he's planned it.

Coco drops the rod and darts over to help untangle her. You'll have to do better than that, says Roxy, grinning at him.

He stands fake-contrite, head down, then offers the net to Coco. You try it.

She throws it straight into the surf, not the backhanded way girls usually have, but with serious skill. It lands ten yards out and sinks. She pulls it tight and wades into the water, shoes and clothes and all. You idiot, says Roxy but she follows her.

He at least kicks off his boots before he splashes in. Cold!

The women are frozen in front of three or four flapping fish. Nice work, he says.

Roxy presses Coco's arm. Leave it, she says, but Coco doesn't. She steps in farther, up to her waist, she grabs the biggest fish and works to untangle its fins from the net. Roxy starts talking fast: In Tahiti they fish with flashlights at night and eat what they catch with their hands.

You've been to Tahiti?

We've seen a documentary, says Coco before Roxy can answer. She quickly opens a fish with her fingernails, guts it and eats it while it's still flapping. A kind of wild sushi, she explains, gnawing at the barely dead fish.

Tim stands there, mouth open.

No, he won't try it.

You're sure? asks Coco again, holding up a tail, as if she's testing him.

He catches them exchanging a look. Another time, he says.

Yeah, says Roxy. It's getting dark, I think we should head back.

He doesn't say no.

Water streams from their shoes all the way to the terminal, and he can see Roxy shivering. Trying to keep her warm, he puts his arm around her shoulder, and she doesn't shake it off. He notes how much he's attracted to: the ripple of muscle in her upper arms, the glitter of her eyes, the long fingers, the mysterious torso.

He's got to cut bait or—

He raises his hand to the back of his neck, considering the problem. That's the first time he feels the bumpy rise, the itchiness of new growth, a scaly something under his fingers.

Chapter 15

WE'RE DRUNK on wine leftover from the picnic, slouched on Roxy's bed. *The Bachelor*'s reality show blares from her screen, and somebody has five seconds to apologize. I love it, she says, he sounds just like Tim.

The guy isn't what he seems, I say. Are you really watching this? Get with the program. Love falls apart, love gets sued. He promises one thing and then does something else.

My favorite show, she groans.

Have you ever seen a harpy turn down raw fish? I ask her. Tim can't be harpy.

Tim's a harpy! He's a smart harpy and didn't betray his harpiness by eating it. And he loved the beach. I'm going to do what I need to do, she sings back at me: It's Fate.

No, it's not, I say. What are we, clocks or clouds?

Clocks, clocks, clocks, she shrieks. Fate!

Don't say that, it's way too human. I pin her down with the comforter. We don't know, we just don't know. You laid such a lovely egg last time, remember? Losing it was so traumatic I think you have amnesia about what happened.

Yes, she says, that cat.

Tiger. Oh, sis, I say, I have to get you out of here. I'm going to tell them at work that we're quitting.

No. She fights off the covers, looking stricken, and sits up. Nobody knows. He totally pretends that there's nothing going on most of the time.

They say if you have a cat in the same house as a bird in a cage, the cat will stalk the bird all its life, until one of them is dead.

Roxy pushes her hair out of her face. Coco, she says, what happened in France?

Nothing really. I mean, nothing unusual.

I see, says Roxy. She scoots to the edge of the bed and points out the window. What's that?

What? I say. I lean forward a little. That van? I checked that guy out a long time ago, a cell tower adjuster, he won't be here forever.

Yeah, I can read. She gives me a hard tell-me-the-truth stare.

Look, I'm not dumb. Do you think I'd stick around if I thought I was in danger?

Roxy nods.

Chapter 16

NAMED AS a defendant for the *State v. Collins*, I have to attend the hearing. In any other circumstance except protecting Roxy, I would have flown off right after having been written up. Courts are one fight I like to avoid. Why, I haven't hung around in a judicial situation since Herod. Now there was a child murderer, executing all those baby boys. The saying went that it was better to be Herod's pig than his son, given that he murdered three of his own.

My turn. Before anyone can object, I show the court blown-up prints of my cell phone pictures: the baby's burns, the state of the house, two half-dressed parents, sprawled.

Foul, cry the parents and their attorney, and even my attorney, who hates surprises, who spent the twenty minutes before we entered the courtroom prepping me to keep my mouth shut and to just answer the questions. He cautioned me not to produce the pictures, they made me seem too aggressive, exactly what he wanted to avoid.

But the judge has seen them.

Thank goodness they can't bring in the baby. He'd be in tiptop shape by now, having spent three weeks in temporary care. Nobody hurt this kid, the parents would say in their defense. Does this look like a kid a parent has hurt?

Stewie couldn't come in and back me up with his meth-making photos. Tim put him on an emergency intervention involving a domestic dispute and the police want him to help pull the family apart. He's the expert. Does Tim want me out of his way? At least he doesn't show, thank god, no damning departmental words of wisdom from him, so it's just my testimony against theirs. Did I threaten the plaintiff? Of course not. Thank you, says the judge. Then the parents come forward. They don't say they saw a woman with wings, they say I was "not in compliance." The judge pages through their mental health report, affidavits from responsible people—a teacher, their landlord, a previous employer—who attest to their competence, or at least past competence. The couple looks ill at ease in their "competent" clothing.

The thing is, I don't fear them saying they saw a woman bird, which would sink them for sure, nor do I really fear losing my job; the department needs me too much. I am, however, curious about the outcome of this face-off. I contemplate the fate of the innocent baby, the chances of it being all bad, while sitting outside the courtroom for however long it takes, until the door finally opens, and the agency lawyer, the child's lawyer, the appellants and the judge file out.

Despite my photos, the judge has decided the parents need another chance. I should feel relieved I wasn't implicated, says the agency lawyer. The couple, of course, is delighted to have won against me. I smile and congratulate them while they gloat. The judge starts to gossip with their lawyer. The agency's lawyer rolls his eyes at me. Flashing those pictures turned the judge against us, he says.

Humans. So much is done in spite—like the judge making me their point of contact. Great, I still have to visit.

I'm nearly pulling out my feathers by the time I get home. My sister doesn't help. She's on the couch with her phone in her lap, ga-ga, waiting for Tim to call.

Why doesn't he call? she says the second after she utters her sorries about the judge's decision. We saw him at the zoo and then all afternoon at the island, not to mention every day at the office. I'm not avoiding him that much. He's hot and cold, right? Like a faucet.

More games. I slice open a new bag of sunflower seeds. He could be busy.

The Collins female is delighted to open the door Monday morning when I arrive to return the baby. She's kitted out in a mother costume like the one she wore to court: a skirt, shoes, brushed hair, and a smirk. They don't have a crib so I build a little fort of cast-off clothes around him in case he manages to push himself to the edge of the couch. You've got to get a real bed, I say to her. It's a requirement.

Make me.

What was the judge thinking? The next day when I come to pick him up, I find the baby crying on the floor, his shirt on backward, and little pricks of blue and smears of blood all up and down on his arm, as if someone had been trying to tattoo him with a pushpin.

Stewie doesn't ask about what's going on when I bring the baby back to the van. I don't even have to show him the little pricks; he sees a look on my face that stops all comment.

At lunch I tell Stewie I have to go collect something. He waves me off—he's doing his kale thing again, steaming it in the microwave, and he's hungry.

Back at the Collins house, I push my way past a pile of socks, bedding, an extension cord, a filthy bra, a broken piece of furniture, and a pushed-over side table to the parents in the far room. They're arguing over what size toaster to order online.

I take off my jacket.

Chapter 17

SMOTE? AGAIN? Now you can't stay and help me for sure, screeches my sister, way-aggravated, more-than-furious.

We'll see.

She presses her fists against her head as if she's going to explode. You're just trying to screw things up and drag me away from Tim.

If you want to have this egg and Tim turns out to be a harpy, he'll find you. I hold up both hands, the international signal for *relax*. By now I know not to leave any evidence at the scene of the crime. Lure them outside, fly them up, drop them—not even a fingerprint. And anyway, the story is that the parents weren't home when I picked up the baby, and now he's back in the hands of the court.

Somebody must have seen them. Or you.

Yeah, I say. Who? They were drug dealers specializing in not being seen.

My sister sighs. The baby's an orphan now.

A foster family has to be able to do better. I've checked

out the system, at least here it's not too bad. I open my computer, ostensibly to check my email, but it's more to shield me from her anger. I'm not plucking the baby out of a nest in the Alps and taking him to my aerie.

I remember that. She puts her head in her hands.

I stop reading the screen and look up. What's the problem now?

If the baby turns out to be an abusive parent the way they usually do when they have parents like that, she screeches in her bird voice, really upset—you'll have to kill it too. Is it too much to wait for human justice?

I press *Save*.

My sister moves to the chair beside me. You shriek in your sleep, she says to me.

It's upsetting, to get this wound up, I say. You think I like it?

She goes on about how happy she was all this time, in this town, with good work to do. I could've stayed here maybe another twenty years! She's a weeper all right. She keeps her face turned away from me.

It's not my fault, I say, crooning to her. It's not my fault.

The other day, she says, sniffling, when I went out to the street to get a little air I thought he was behind me, about to make his move, but now I think it was just a shrike, flying really low.

Such longing. I pat her back, just above the wings.

My sister twists around. You killed again, she says.

So give me a medal, I say. The baby is saved.

Chapter 18

CAUGHT YOU.

Robinson repositions the camera and plays it back, switching on another as backup.

No. Still not clear. Every so often the window goes up and then there's this blur and whoever's there is not there anymore. He doesn't know how they do it. For a while he thought the bad images were because of his eyes, old age or too many French fries or he blinked—but it's got to be the shutter speed. He wishes he had one of those cameras you could tuck into a book or a suitcase, but the resolution on those isn't so great and he needs resolution. Yesterday, watching Coco go off to work, he dropped his lens cap in the foyer of social services—he might as well have dropped his trousers. By the time he found the lens cap behind a hat rack, she was gone.

What he needs for this type of surveillance is the STS 80 spotting scope. With video coupling, it can find moving targets a lot quicker than this piece of shit. But he can't afford an upgrade. The big bonus he received for the Kardashians is supposed to be for a new roof, and celebrity gigs are few and far between anymore, drying up with all the cheap bugs you can buy now online, like the one he bought for the dog. But why does he need a new roof when his wife and kids have left him?

He stares at the front of his camera as if it had an answer, his mind hems and haws. Maybe he can borrow a lens from the office. Although he thinks it's Interpol that's behind this job, he suspects it's more likely the FBI and they're stingy. He would love it if it were the NSA because they have the best equipment, but they only hire people with a math degree.

At least Coco hasn't gone back to the zoo. He didn't mention in the report how she tricked him at the exit. He tried using a drone last week. She raised the window and pretended to water the flower box and down the drone went. He's beginning to feel some spite.

He phones his neighbor to find out if the dog walker really takes the dog on walks on the street or just sits in the backyard. This is a new neighbor, the old one loved to report on everything.

The neighbor says he's not a voyeur, thank you very much, and hangs up.

Oh, well.

Speaking of which, he keeps wishing she'd let that bathrobe of hers fall open, though she's not actually his type. Not that she'd pay much attention to him, being so young

and attractive, with the long legs and all, and the nice lipstick and the way she purses her lips at him whenever she
goes by the car. His type is—what is it?

He's separated. Like 50 percent of married people are
separated, how can it be that so many people don't know
their type? Or is there a separated type?

He has his fantasies, something he never had with
his wife. Coco is like having his own goddess. He's down
here, she's up there. Being a possible criminal makes her
more mysterious and godlike, even if she just stares out the
window or goes to work. And he cares about her. Already
he's starting to worry whenever she goes out driving the
car. It's such a wreck, he's sure it will break down. Would
he jump out of the van to help her? Wouldn't that speed up
the inquiry?

At least she's not calling the cops. That would be spite.

Yesterday after he picked up the dog, he followed her
to the grocery. He was disguised of course, in a street crew
hard hat and orange vest. No camera. There was a little drizzle, and the dog was really crazy, barking and barking, so he
couldn't have gotten a steady shot anyway. She just tossed
her head when she passed them and walked faster, this
funny shuffle she gets whenever she wants to really move.
Makes her hips wiggle. Nothing you would notice if she
were just strolling. As if her shoes are bothering her. She's
been nervous lately too, looking over her shoulder, chewing
her nails. Something on her mind.

When he turned around, the dog was in perfect

conformation. Must be the kids, screwing around with all the effort he put in turning the mutt into a bird dog. They're the ones who need training.

Anyway, the barking made him a little conspicuous.

Switching the camera to record, he leans back in his chair. Maybe he's obsessed with having the right equipment like his wife has always accused him, pleading for the roof, yes, maybe he is an equipment nut, and maybe he doesn't appreciate his dog when he barks too much now and then, but he's also only human. At least the job has its pleasures. He likes to watch women behind curtains women's behinds women bending over the sill the tops of their na-nas showing their shoulders with their nighties sliding off women in the dark and their soft skin women watching women women women.

Chapter 19

REAGAN UNEARTHS the many mirrors her mother had stored in the basement of the faux eighteenth-century chateau that the new aviary is being attached to. She had been entranced by these mirrors as a small child. Large enough that she could see her whole body, the ripples in the glass took her elsewhere, away from her mother and her infernal taxidermy. Her pet budgie—she was allowed to keep one live bird—had a mirror of its own attached to its cage. About a month after it was installed, the bird starved to death because it kept vomiting its food to feed its image. Although her mother offered to stuff the bird, she refused and buried it in a shoebox with its mirror—that was his true love—and begged her mother to get rid of the big ones. Saving her mother from a bad case of narcissism?

Standing in front of one now, she wonders at how much she has come to resemble her mother: long-necked, slit eyed, and thin-haired, the better to match the birds too. Her father had been stout and square chinned, a bottle of a person in the wedding picture she'd found stuck inside another mirror's backing. He left her mother before she was born, having been forced into marriage after her mother claimed he made her pregnant. Forced wasn't quite the right word when she reviewed the situation with adult scrutiny, because he'd also departed with half her mother's fortune. The marriage and divorce generated such great hate that when Reagan traveled to Europe to meet him, he took one look at her and slammed the door shut. She must have been the same age as her mother when they were wed and her face too similar.

Nothing personal.

She takes the elevator out of the basement. She'll get the workmen to recycle the mirrors. Surely they would be in demand somewhere, perhaps the same place that is taking most of the dusty birds? As a child, she'd cringed under all those birds staring down at her and wondered about her mother's emulation of them, their very deadness. But who could understand a parent? She had no idea collecting could be such a passion until her mother was disposing of a diorama that contained five tiny hummingbird eggs shaped exactly like Tic Tacs. On her own, Reagan discovered owls make globe-like eggs, and that sandpipers lay pointy eggs shaped like raindrops. Collecting eggs became a side interest and is now central, perhaps even an obsession. The more interesting eggs are illegal to obtain, though she knows that a good number of the club members, serious birders, have also jumped the rail, finding such eggs irresistible.

Whispered clues for where one might find their nests are always circulating.

Birds don't just fly in a window.

She opens one.

The work of preserving the taxidermy collection and many of the rarer habitats in the wild is so complex. Upgrades to the exhibits—shifting creatures in their various difficult-to-clean-and-improve environments, not to mention her own expensive renovations—have been costly. Besides, feathers and teeth fall out of specimens, mold insinuates itself, and wings break off. Her grandfather's railroad money had been nearly exhausted by her mother's collecting, let alone hers. She will have to raise vast sums to continue adequate conservation, really a gigantic waste of time when one's interests lie elsewhere, and, of course, one's time is limited.

No one lives forever, stuffed or otherwise.

Six months earlier, Reagan found this amazing picture on the internet. Of course it could have been photoshopped—a woman with wings—but it wasn't, she had had it analyzed. One of the better photo forensic teams worked on the posting to verify it and discovered the location and identity of the creature. To her great surprise, the harpy was nesting nearby, a lucky—no, serendipitous—coincidence. It was her destiny to deal with it professionally. At first she thought all she needed was an anonymous idiot to establish proximity and take notes to confirm her hypothesis, but then there was all the business about securing the job for him, enduring his complaints, paying his ever-increasing invoices, and reviewing the sloppy results. She now wants more, much more, but he doesn't seem adequately qualified. Still, she can't start over. The elixir alone cost half a year's interest on her trust.

Is she so wrong in pursuing the bird? Everyone wants animals properly treated, and with shrinking habitats, everyone should be kind to them. Even Hitler was kind to animals. He had that dog, Blondi. But he poisoned it. Not that she is Hitler. Far from it. Exterminating a species through taxidermy is never the best approach—but who knows how many harpies are still at large? Or there may be flocks that have been ignored for centuries, even abused. Passenger pigeons exemplify the problem. They were once the most numerous birds in the world. Flocks of passenger pigeons darkened the sky for hours, their wing beats so loud you couldn't hear yourself talk, and after they poured themselves down to the ground to feed on acorns and beechnuts, and sometimes crops, they left droppings everywhere, whitening the bare earth like snow. She'd heard that trees would fall from the weight of so many nests. But to kill the pigeons, all you had to do was wave a pole at the low-flying ones and down they went. They were shot, trapped with nets, torched in their roosts, smothered with burning sulfur. Hunters attacked them with rakes, pitchforks, and potatoes, poisoned them with whiskey-soaked corn. Eventually trains transported hunters to their last nesting sites, and that was that. If you restrict the killing, people will lose their jobs, went the argument. Martha, the last passenger pigeon in the world, refused to lay and expired at the age of twenty-nine in the Cincinnati zoo. Visitors threw sand at her to make her move, but she wouldn't.

If a creature once so ubiquitous can vanish, imagine how quickly the rare ones disappear. And considering that harpies might kill people—a big predator like that—she could be saving lives by taking her in. Why, the human fatality rate with harpies, she imagined, could be as high as the cassowary's. By intervening in the harpy's haphazard habitat and providing one that is more congenial to the species, she would also prove that she is a very generous and farsighted scientist. Of course if the harpy should lay an egg—

Chapter 20

AT THE very end of the lunchroom—enough linoleum for a hundred truants—sits Chris, bored at a cafeteria table, skateboard beside him. He's bitten his after-school peanut butter and jelly into the shape of a gun and his carrot stick into a knife, his Jell-O's poisoned with so many salt packets it looks like snow, and his cucumber slices haven't been touched. So much for the free meal. Usually the kids are hungry, very hungry, and they eat everything we give them, but he must be too upset and nervous. That's my generous assessment, not the one that says he's defiant, the one in his record. It's the third time we've pulled him in.

Kids scream in the gym just beyond him, having fun. Why exactly do I have to wait here for a ride? he asks.

The rules, I say. I look around, I actually look over my shoulder. I'm a little paranoid after my smote, I'm used to getting away, not sticking around. You're not into eating? I ask.

Too many vegetables.

I take a seat next to him and pull his hand to me and open it. Here we have your future, I say, touching a line on his hand. More vegetables.

He can't wiggle out of my grip. With his other hand, he rolls his skateboard closer. He says, I have no future.

Is that what your father tells you? I release him.

He scoots away, stands up, drops his skateboard and stomps on it so one end slaps into his free hand.

Your dad says that to scare you into obeying him. I grab his hand again and point at his palm. I don't see anything about the end of the world here. Not this year or the next.

He jerks his hand away.

May I have my notebook back? And the pen?

You think you know everything, he says. He'd nicked my notebook earlier in the day, when I passed him in the hall. Here, he says, digging it out of his backpack and spinning it toward me, taking a seat again. *Let that be a lesson to him,* he says in my voice. You wrote about somebody a lot like me.

I write in code, I say.

You don't like my father. And I didn't take your pen.

I do like him. How could I not like him? He puts up with you. You should really eat your food, I say, tucking the notebook into my bag. And I was sure I had a pen.

He doesn't pick up the fork or the spoon, he scratches his head. Who's Roxy? What kind of name is that? You wrote it in your book.

She works here. Roxy is a nickname for Ocypetes, which means *swift* in Greek.

He bounces up, he skateboards in quick tight circles. I read if you swim in this Greek river you forget everything, he says.

How do you know about that river—some video game?

He studies me, rolling past. One grade I was in. They gave you bunches of classic comics if you could read two words put together.

What was that—fifth? Sixth grade? How's your spelling?

He wrinkles his forehead and recites, The "eese" family: geese, meese, niece. Spelling is my worst, he says. Reading is different.

I take out my notebook and another pen, and he flinches. Okay, okay. I'm writing positive things: *Very ambitious reader.*

He grins; he can't help it.

Now, if you could have anything in the whole wide world—

What a strange question, says the angle of his head. I repeat it. Kids usually instantly know the answer, and it reveals something important. He doesn't disappoint. A silver belt buckle, he says, just like that. Hard to find for kids, my dad says.

Your dad won't get you one?

Expensive, he says.

I pull at my jacket where it pinches my flexing wings. What does a belt buckle tell me about him? He's got a cowboy fetish? He's a conspicuous consumer, wanting to show off a precious metal? Confusing, but I'm going to need all the friends I can get if anybody finds out about the Collinses. I tell him I will try to find one of those buckles. Right now, I'm going to get you a drink of water. They must have something in the kitchen. I crane my neck around and see the kitchen's closed.

Ha, he says, more ketchup and mustard packets is all there is.

I hold up my hands. Want to beat me in cards? I bet there's a deck in a drawer somewhere in the room. We have time. Stewie won't be here for another ten minutes.

The kids in the next room laugh even louder, scream at some joke we can't quite hear. He shifts on his board, he shakes his head *No-no-no* to the cards.

So go with the others, I say. Forget the rules. I'll get you when he shows up.

Chapter 21

TIM SCRUBS the back of his neck with a brush and much soap. It's still rough. Terrible eczema or something. He's decided to take a break from wearing this perfume or whatever Reagan said he needed so much of. It must've soaked into his skin and into his system and is causing this outbreak. It's also causing him to have the hots for her all the time although there's been no roll in the hay, just a few kisses. He'd rather err on the side of caution in that regard. Getting all bonded and emotional has never worked out for him, plus this physical stuff seems hard to turn off—and she might, what, eat him?

Reagan rags him first thing, calling right after he steps out of the shower. Talk about a harpy! The DNA is good, she says. You'll have to get on it.

I was very close to confirmation just yesterday, he says.

Tear off her blouse. It's easy, says Reagan. A fit of passion.

What does she know about passion? He towels off. Roxy's been avoiding me, he says as if that's a defense, but she of course doesn't buy that, she says they have a contract and hangs up.

He's told her nothing about the ferry trip. He collects more money if he doesn't rush it, he doesn't attract attention, he keeps the courtship exciting, he does his job with the kids. It turns out he likes the job. It's his chance to get even with his parents, that mother of his who made him walk all night, sometimes in the rain, until whatever guy paid her. He was only ten years old and he didn't know anybody with parents who would take him in. What he did have was a drunk dad who took the money she earned and beat her afterward, and then beat him worse for not "protecting" her.

He read in *Social Service Worker* that a parent a day gets offed by their kids. He's surprised it isn't more. Apparently it's all about having a gun in the house. Thank god his dad never had one, or at least not one he ever knew about. He won't carry a gun himself. He has anger, plenty of anger from childhood on up, and he's afraid of it. Getting a record would put him in quite another position.

Of course he could be falling for Roxy for real, scent or no scent. That would be a change. Or else it's this job where he has to help people all the time—uh, empower them. When he called his ex to tell her he was sending a birthday present to his son, she was like *You sure? You never did that before.*

Tim drives to today's meeting with Reagan whistling. He can whistle a lot better lately.

———

Reagan flips through photos of the new construction the contractors are doing on her country property. It will be the most beautiful aviary in the three-state region, she boasts. So big it can fit condors. The village planning commission's been notified of its unusual size, and the state has approved it. For avian specimen safety, is what I told them.

Tim's standing in her office on the third floor of the Club because she hasn't asked him to sit down. Anyway, it's a good sign they're meeting here instead of the main area—she's starting to trust him. Behind her desk are shelves filled with little chalices of pink or blue-speckled or green eggs collected or traded from all over the world, according to the cards propped up in front of them.

The plans show a private area too, she says, where the creatures can't be observed. All the animals have them now, even the chimps, with stools and a table the specimens can eat on, if they choose. A ball to play with, a board for scratching, and who knows—canaries like whalebone for their whistles, she says, maybe something similar? There's so much we don't know about them, she says, folding her computer closed.

She drinks wine and drives, he says.

Reagan comes out from behind her desk. Should a priceless painting be allowed to fall into the hands of the billionaire who has the wall space, or the connoisseur who would truly appreciate it? Should such a specimen go free and endanger herself and any possible offspring? You would be doing the world a favor to bring her in.

Collect her? he asks, taking a step back. Kidnapping is expensive.

Kidnapping? she shrieks in a club-like whisper. It's a bird. An endangered bird.

Last I heard, all you wanted was physical confirmation, and I'm getting to it. He removes an invisible bit of lint from his jacket. Would you display her nude?

The room has a tropical heat, adjusted for the exhibits. She looks over her glasses at him. Roxy, as you call her, has feathers.

Probably not so many.

You'll see. The woman laughs. You're a diaper-on-the-gorilla man?

I'm just your go-between, he says. I'm the paid thug. He wants more money in proportion to how many feathers have sprouted on him but he doesn't tell her about that yet, he'll move on that later. After all, she might want to collect him.

Here's a new invoice for up to today, he says, withdrawing a slip of paper from a pocket. With overtime.

Are you seeing her evenings? she asks, looking over his columns. I mean, are you actually cultivating a relationship?

I am friendly, he says with an edge. That's what it requires. Nice earrings, he says, to distract her from his numbers.

She frowns, touching the tips of the two porcelain eggs

dangling from her ears, reviewing the bill. It was a flat fee we agreed on.

He says nothing. It's like poker, you can't back down from an invoice.

She comes around her desk with purse in hand. Are you going to do this job the way I want it or not?

Hearing the tone of her voice, his brain goes completely combative—he's got to be hard-ass. It's a job, he barks. A rental van with no windows for the kidnapping, maybe netting or sedatives if you want me to get fancy, detailing afterward to prevent fingerprint detection, etc. He doesn't tell her he'll borrow transport from social services and pocket most of the fee.

She produces a checkbook. I can write it off, she says. No more PayPal. My accountant mentioned a tax advantage if I wrote the checks right.

No, he says. He must have cash for the kidnapping, she's crazy to leave a trail, taxes or whatever. He tells her there's an ATM in town where he can meet her.

She seems put off by the professionalism she's paying for. If you insist. She tucks her checkbook back into the purse. The other man I wanted to hire had credentials, she says, with sound avian experience, a collector himself. I didn't hire him because I suspected he would never hand over the goods. She leans back against the desk. I'm not going to have that problem with you, am I?

I'll be glad when this is finished, he says and takes a

closer look at the exhibit behind her. You don't have any more taxidermied birds up here? I'd have thought you'd need quite a few to study.

I'd have feared is what he stopped himself from saying.

Oh, no, she says. The acquisition of live specimens is more interesting and a bit more of a challenge than stuffing the dead ones the way my mother preferred. But really, I just want the eggs. To show their origins. Aren't they beautiful?

He's relieved. It's one thing to kidnap a bird and another to turn over your lover for taxidermy. He peers through the glass, he says: The blue ones with the spots look like the Easter kind.

Yes, yes, she says. Very discerning. You've seen that shot of their wingspread I found on the internet?

That and the Loch Ness monster. He turns toward the window, away from her and her fancy executive office exhibit.

She clears her throat. I need you to collect her.

At least she's using a Honey-won't-you-do-this-for-me voice. He holds up his hands. Right. I don't know how to do my job.

Your attraction, such as it is, will wane otherwise.

That's what you think.

She smiles as if he's joking. You haven't finished your last write-up. You're behind.

I read your email, he says. I just haven't gotten around to it. This cover-up job is a time-suck, and when I went into this work four months ago, I didn't realize I'd have so many cases to keep track of.

Listen, she says, tapping on the table, the more detail we have on her, the better the collection. But no bird traps. They'll ruin her conformation. Her bone structure—her figure, she says, when he stares at her blankly. Rare birds are not so different from, say, diamonds, she says. These particular eggs are about as valuable. She points at a clutch of round pink eggs on a high shelf behind her, displayed in a locked clear acrylic box. We have no idea how much hers will bring.

He peers at the acrylic, pulls his lip in doubt. This is the third time you've told me.

No, really. People sometimes take years staking out the nests. Somebody spent nearly a month monitoring a cliff in subarctic Manitoba for these amazing Arctic tern eggs.

Subarctic?

You're lucky with this one in that she has such a congenial habitat. Reagan rummages again in her purse. Yes, oology has its adventures. Lord Rothschild was once the most famous oologist in the world and left the most eggs. He also had a carriage drawn by zebras and a worm named after him.

That's ambition for you.

The worm was just a side thing. She produces a key from her purse that she uses to open the small smoked-glass cabinet next to the exhibit case. Here's a bit more of that solution.

Doesn't mean he has to use it, he doesn't say. He pockets the bottle.

It's a hostile world out there, she says. She lets her purse fall open, replacing the key, so he gets a glimpse of a small gun, and he knows she saw that glimpse. A rare specimen shouldn't be allowed to fend for itself, she goes on. You'll be doing her a favor.

She unbolts the office door to let him out. The floor is like Fort Knox. He imagines her country house and aviary will be just as secure.

Good security, he says.

And if she's not collected, she says, the world will be deprived of an entire species.

Once through the side door and down onto the street, he flexes his shoulders as if throwing off her demands. Or the back of his neck is bothering him.

He knows for his own sake he has to complete the job.

An hour later, it's so warm he opens his office window, but in minutes he can't stand hearing the skateboard roar by one more time. He throws up the screen and sticks his head out: Take that over to the park!

The kid gives him the finger.

As if the sound of the skateboard is a bird caught in his room, he flails his arms out the window. Hey—I'll put it in your file, he shouts. Go somewhere else.

The kid stops to shout back: I'm waiting for Coco.

So wait under a rock. He stands in front of the window,

hands clenched. The kid stands there too. He's about the age of his own, probably. Not that his son would pay any attention to him either. Why should he? They never even lived in the same house. He slams the window hard, and then he locks it.

Anger. It escapes him so easily.

The skateboard begins its thunder again.

He runs his hands over his face. So maybe he gets a little carried away. He is a little tense. His heart is pounding. The job—that other one—is a lot of pressure, the work here is almost a relief.

He has a batch of files to check against the digital scans for validation before shredding them. Closed cases. *Do no harm* is the motto but closed cases always suggest harm. Cases are followed and cases develop, but they often resolve as untidily as they come into being. This is what he learns ticking so many "dead" or "suicide" boxes on the spreadsheet.

Outside, the skateboard grinds on.

Chapter 22

I'M LAUGHING. The guy from the surveillance van is dragging around a camera with a lens the size of a howitzer. He can hardly rest it on the table without it tipping, and he's already spilled half his coffee on his—what?—unregistered student disguise? A button-down shirt, sweats, and a stick-on mustache. Still, it must be great to be out of that van. Look at him lumber over to the garbage to unload his trash, his sneaking between tables to make it harder for me to see him—whoops, there goes the sugar container.

At least now he's settled. I give him a nod.

No one's figured out the situation with the Collinses yet. Maybe I'll get away with it. That happens about half the time. Worrying about possible scenarios, I've fallen behind with the interminable reports and now have to catch up at night. I prefer the café scene to the office anyway. It makes me think I'm back in France, except for the weak coffee and the stale roll. Vestigial behavior on my part, my territorial instincts, like a dog trying to bury a bone in the couch.

I'm barely seated when my phone rings.

I'm not surprised that it's Chris's father. The kid must've copied whatever interesting information he could find in my notebook before giving it back, like my cell number. His father's asking me if I can stop by sometime soon, very soon, how about sometime this weekend? He can't get Chris to eat when he's home all day, and he's getting more and more wound up at night, talking all the time, not sleeping. If I could just take him for a few hours. A change of scene. Chris likes you, he respects you.

He's at the end of his rope.

I seem to remember he had plenty of rope. I'm a little tired, the new routine of keeping up with work is grinding, even for a harpy who seldom sleeps. I am thinking he has some kind of date and he doesn't want his kid around. Chris is a fine boy, or fine enough with some supervision. After he hangs up I text him: *Chris won't starve over the weekend.*

How were you punished as a child is the first question I always ask a client, says Stewie. You'd be surprised how many parents give themselves away, how few show any imagination. That Collins woman had a father who threatened her with a tattoo gun whenever she made too much noise. That's in her file.

I hadn't made that connection. I look out at the traffic filling the skies with carbon, its own punishment. I myself was very seldom punished—I ran free as a bird. And you?

Stewie is not prone to talk about his growing up. He says he's heard so many say they wished somebody would have helped them when they were kids. He thinks it's a gift we are giving them. We make a few mistakes now and then, but mostly we don't, he says. He sighs and stops at the light. Coco, he says, what a jazzy name. You know what Stewie means?

I shake my head.

It means mixed-up, carrots, potatoes, meat, gravy. I'm Black, white, Native American, Cuban—I've got everything. You ought to envy me.

I do, I say. You're the future, so long as airplanes keep flying everyone around all the time.

I love flying, he says.

I cock my head. You ever see the color of the skin under a bird's feathers?

Sometimes purple, he says. Depends on the breed, exercise, age, diet. Younger poultry has less fat under the skin, which can cause a bluish cast, and yellow skin might be because of marigolds in the feed.

Uh, Stewie, I say. You sure know a lot about birds.

Stewie yawns as if I am making him nervous. Okay, well, I'll tell you—I raised pigeons when I was young. We lived in a tenement where the roof was open and you could keep cages. There wouldn't have been so many to keep if we hadn't given them and all the wild ones the perfect habitat.

What happened to them—did somebody let them out?

He nods, tapping our next address into the GPS.

But they would've come back, I say. They were pigeons.

The super plugged in sonic repellent. You know, the kind that emits bird distress calls and sounds that predators make? We watched them fly around overhead, unable to roost, just out of reach, and eventually they flew somewhere else. Or starved to death, given how much pigeons are used to being fed by people.

He makes a left. Get this, he says, if you're poor and Black or Brown, forget it, people think you're an animal. If you're a poor white with a mental problem, that also might get you animal status. People don't care much about animals, let alone birds. They should just fly away.

I understand, I say. So many people.

He turns down the road that runs past Chris's place. The apartment front light is left on as if somebody went out late and forgot about it. Wasting electricity! says Stewie.

I tell him the dad phoned over the weekend. I said I'd drop by.

Stewie nods. It's your call. He's not on the list.

I look at the crawling traffic in front of us. Maybe later.

Stewie edges into a better lane. You know how the mother bird runs away from the nest if you walk too close to it? It looks like abandonment but it's really protective—the bird hopes you'll go after her instead of the young. I mean, she's where the most protein is.

I am familiar with the strategy, I say.

He makes another left.

So when a mother gets really uncooperative, he says, you just have to assume maybe the guy she lives with is going to beat her up or the kids if he hears that she's getting help from you. At the very least, the guy might not give her money to buy food, or he'll poison the cat or keep the kids up late to get back at her. This one guy forced his kid to run on a treadmill until he passed out. This first case is like that.

What you mean is, the mother might be in jeopardy herself.

Two cars turning right from different lanes almost collide. Stewie's got good reflexes. He doesn't flinch.

Look around the house for obvious things like kick marks or holes punched in the wall. I'll park a block away so we don't advertise our visit. Sometimes if a family knows you're coming, they'll put a towel over the door to hide any evidence. You might have to feel a child's bedding to see if it's soaked with urine or stare into the toilet to see what failed to flush. The consequences of getting it wrong are really huge—kids locked in the bedroom whole weekends without food or water, their mouths stuffed with pantyhose. I had a case where a baby left a bloodstain on the ceiling where he was thrown. Not many caseworkers would think to look up.

He slows down in front of a very nice three-story house set back far from the street with a big yard ending in foresty bits, then he finds a space two blocks past it. Seriously? I say, looking at the intake.

Abuse knows no demographics. The kids were found wandering around by a neighbor who called us.

You're opening the door this time.

Every one of the walls inside has punched-in holes. We're rethinking the plumbing, says the mother, a tall brunette in not-so-nice stained loungewear with a whiskery pony-tail pulled to one side. A dog sounds big in a distant room, then it bounds in to check us out. Shshshsh, she commands, quiet, but the dog barks louder. Hushing him, she tells us nothing's wrong with her kids, it was really a mistake of the neighbor's. Surely he confused her kids with someone else's. The kids—there are three of them—sit silent under a huge-screen TV that's broadcasting an age-inappropriate soap. While the mother leads the barking dog back into the other room and Stewie scouts the kitchen, I look a little closer.

The younger girl has a small cut and a bruise on her face. I ask the child if I can touch her bruise and it turns out to be a smear of eyebrow pencil, and there's yellow makeup applied in a swath under one of the eyes of the other kids. The mother made sure the neighbors saw them looking bad, I say to Stewie who's just returned.

He's checking some boxes on his form. Hmmmm, he says.

Can Coco have a look around while we talk? he asks as soon as the mother reappears. It'll only take a couple of minutes.

Her eyes flit to another door and then to us.

Paperwork, says Stewie, as if he's apologizing.

She takes a few steps toward the kids, she takes a step back and says okay.

I stalk further into the house. The punched-in walls, the makeup? I'm pretending to tie my shoe, looking under the bed when I crane around and spot a nanny-cam in the corner of the ceiling. Does she get watched even when he's away? I check the bathroom. I'm pushing aside a towel beside the toilet to see if it's hiding anything when a big man rips back the shower curtain, screaming: My house! and swings a baseball bat at me, but it gets mixed up in the curtain, and he smacks the tiles. Then, in another wild swing, he breaks the mirror over the vanity. I'm out of there fast, chairs topple in the living room, the man shouting behind me something about the kids' father.

I don't launch my feathers or talons, that makes a crazy crazier, I yell to Stewie to get out, and we sprint down the block together to the van. Stewie has us moving before I can grip the seat cover, and we're passing the front of the house just when the guy bangs out the door. He lets the bat go on the upswing and instead of hitting us, it smashes the side of the car parked in the driveway.

The wife and the kids stand at the door.

Like it happens every day, I say. I hope that's his own car.

Stewie dials 911. When I first started the job, I got one good piece of advice.

What's that?

Wear shoes you can run in.

He gives the particulars while we careen down the street, then a text chimes. It's Chris's father. *Please come Chris @ Plainview Emergency.*

We have to wait for the police, says Stewie.

He doesn't exactly circle the block the first few times, he makes bigger and bigger loops and by the time we return, the guy's car is gone. We park around the corner but in sight of the driveway in case he comes back. Stewie says darn, we should've at least gotten his license plate.

He's full of it. We're not enforcement, not really even investigation. But I say nothing. We listen to Motown really low, the beat strangely complementing my nerves. Stewie complains about the first mostly white Motown group, the Mynah Birds. They were real copycats but they did have Steppenwolf, Buffalo Springfield, the Guess Who, Rick Matthews, Neil Young playing together. That was something.

I nod as if I know.

They were so sure they were going to make it, they had a tape saying "Hello, Ed Sullivan" playing 24/7 in the birdcage so the mynah bird would know what to say when Sullivan called.

And? I am impatient with Stewie trying to distract me. I'm worried about Chris.

Sullivan never did. So much for their TV debut.

The police come rushing down the block five minutes

later. We point at the baseball bat tossed down in the drive-way and they write in their notebooks, dictate into their phones. The whole family's gone.

Stewie's grim, steering the van back into traffic. Cops are not always so good in domestic disputes anyway, he says. Sometimes they blame the victims. She should've kept the kids quiet, that kind of thing. Probably the guy with the bat isn't even related.

Chapter 23

I'LL BE, says Robinson. The cat's out of the bag.

He means the dog. It's pawing the side of the van where his wife shakes her fist at him, her two kids huddling beside her.

He sticks his hand out the window and pets the dog.

I was just walking the dog and I fell on a crack and that's how I got my black eye, she says.

You're supposed to put steak on it.

How can I afford steak?

He won't let her in. He knows who gave her the black eye, and that was her choice. The kids don't look so happy about it though. I'll tell you what, he says, clearing his throat as if it's his conscience. Here's all the cash I've got on me. He empties his wallet.

She takes whatever little he offers. Not the card?

Not the card. Do you think I'm that dumb?

The boy grabs the money out of her hand. Even he doesn't trust me, she says, and starts crying.

Look, don't make a scene. I'm working here. The suspect should be showing up soon and I have to be ready. He holds up his new lens.

Christ Almighty! That money was supposed to go for the roof, she says, and stomps off with all of them.

Chapter 24

CHRIS'S FATHER is arguing with an intern in the waiting room, looking wild, his glasses broken. He waves at us like *Where have you been?* Instead of stopping, we beeline for Chris, flashing our social work IDs to the guard.

He's strapped to a gurney down at the end of a long hall, his arms limp beneath the restraints but rubbed raw where he's struggled against them. He cracked the windshield with his head, says Stewie reading from the hospital notes. His dad was driving. Broke it out with his head and his hands, somehow with his feet too.

How could that be? I look down at him, his eyes shut, maybe even drugged asleep. He's big for his age but barely a hundred pounds.

It says afterward that his dad got a hammerlock on him and somehow drove down the highway with this popped windshield, Stewie reads, then he honked until Emergency came out.

I guess his dad did need the day off.

Chris looks angelic on the gurney, even with a bandaged nose. Unbelievable. A concussion and a lot of small cuts from the windshield. He seems to have grown another inch in the few days I haven't seen him, his feet almost hang over the end of the bed. Does he understand what's going on? Are his wits scrambled? Is he faking sleep?

Stewie isn't talking truant anymore, he's dog-faced and downcast. He hates it when any of the kids get sick or hurt—fever, broken arm—it's just not fair that they have to be sick on top of what they have to put up with at home. But mental illness? He doesn't have any problem assigning blame as long as it's not the child's fault. He scratches an ear. I'm just going to make a copy of this diagnosis for Chris's report.

Later, I say. Let's go talk to his father.

Before I can get around the gurney, Chris starts to smile.

Wait a minute, Stewie, I say. He must at least recognize our voices.

Still smiling, Chris starts shaking his arm, trying to get the IV needle out.

Okay, okay, I say, pinning him. Use your words.

The kid opens his eyes and clears his throat, he over-enunciates like a drunk: My board is lost.

It says here you had an appointment to see a shrink today, says Stewie. For an emergency evaluation. What happened Sunday that your dad called Coco?

My board isn't really lost, he says. I hate Dad. I hate—

The tendons in Chris's neck tighten, as if he plans to rear

up and hit me with his head like he did the windshield. Where's a nurse? I say.

Stewie heads down the hall to find one.

What else do you hate? I hold his tied-down hand.

Lunch at school. He looks hard at me, one of his eyes twitching. Lunch, he says, lunch, louder and louder.

I guess these meds aren't working so well, says the nurse who rushes in behind Stewie. We'll have to try something else. She dials her phone.

Stewie and I and Chris wait, Chris writhing. My board, he shouts. Fuck!

You've got to believe me, the father shouts just as loud from down the hall. He has his fists balled by the time he makes it to our end. The intern behind him is keeping his distance, a security guard follows.

My wings start to ache. Stewie, god bless him, takes a step forward and puts a hand on the father's shoulder.

I just had to get him here, says the father. I didn't know what else to do so I put him in the car and he broke the windshield. But I got him here.

Chris has both his eyes shut tight.

The intern raises his stethoscope and points it at the father. But I'm not sure you should be the one taking him home.

The father lunges at him.

Outta here, says the security guard. Come back when you're less upset. He shoves him into the hall.

Stewie signals for me to follow.

———

I was once a dandelion kid, says Stewie, driving into the dusk of the city. You just get along and grow up no matter what happens to you. You look good—that nice bright yellow—so nobody digs you up permanently. What was wrong wasn't me.

Stewie is shaken. He's trying to smile, but not the way he smiles when he has kids in the car.

This kid is not a weed, I say.

He's not well, he says. Early onset bipolar, bad, is what the chart said. What can we do?

I shrug, a gesture that's all about the weight of my wings on my back.

Chapter 25

ROBINSON'S WIFE calls and he finally picks up the fourth time. I can't go back to him, she says.

I can't go back, Robinson repeats, making fun of her voice, how shaky she's making it.

We had another little confrontation, she sobs.

Did you?

Look, you've got plenty of room in that van. Help me out here. She inhales, pulling herself together. At least for the afternoon. I have to find somewhere else to stay and the kids aren't helping.

But he has such a nice-looking big house, he says.

She doesn't fill the dead air.

I'll load the kids up with things to watch and homework, she says eventually. They like pizza, you like pizza, and you know they love to go through your spy stuff.

He stares at the corkboard. What's in common with all the victims? Mostly between twenty-four and fifty-five. What else? Cool haircuts? Super-nice cars? Dogs? He makes a noise that isn't exactly yes but isn't really negative. He can never really say no to her, including her decision to move out. The phone call ends with words of gratitude.

Uh-oh. He must've said something positive.

Maybe an hour later, the children—and the dog— climb into the van and it's instant mayhem. Sure, they have enough programming of their own to watch, plus pockets full of candy and bags of chips, but all they want to do is plug and unplug his wires and ask detailed questions. The littlest one especially, the really cute one with a Band-Aid across her cheek who likes to sit on his lap and fool with the dials. Why are you so interested in this channel, she says. There's no program.

The dog starts barking in all the fun. Robinson plugs music into his ears.

Their mother will be gone for hours and hours. Just the way it used to be when they lived together. He'd come home, having worked his tail off for days, sometimes for weeks, and she would rush out the door, saying it was too much with the kids, she needed a break, why didn't he return home sooner? Three children. She could've stopped at one, but she swore she really liked babies, one father at a time. He didn't fall for that and make it number four, and that's really why they split. He forgets how they ever got together—oh, yes, she lived around the corner from one of his stakeouts and one day she took a seat on the bench next to his car, just sat there with her stroller and the kids and wept. He broke protocol and got out and said hello. She said her boyfriend had just left her. Maybe that's what she always says.

The kids are okay as kids, especially now that they're older, though still a financial drain since the support money isn't so good two husbands back, but they are definitely hers and he's fine with that. Cuts down on any argument. Shopping is what she'll tell him she was doing when she gets back, some vague destination you can't argue with. Shopping for another boyfriend is what he thinks.

The eldest, a boy, practices his drum rolls on the metal of one of the recording machines, the next kid cries because her toy has fallen into the battery pit and can't be pulled out, and the last one, with her Band-Aid, just stares at him as if he is a god.

He catches the boy moving the pins around, but then the pizza guy arrives, and he has to take care of that without the dog eating the whole pie and the children spilling coke on the equipment.

It's while he's handing out the slices that Coco exits the building. He plays it cool but he has to tie the shoe of the middle girl and when he gets back to his seat in front, the littlest is licking pizza sauce off the window and the dog is barking to beat the band. Coco is now two feet away, laughing her head off, then she's gone.

He'll get some action, goddammit. Seatbelts on! he yells, strapping in the littlest himself. He tears out of the spot, and the kids start screaming, *Left!* Or, *She's over there.* Or, *Is she that one?* Or, *Stop sign!* He loses her and by the time he makes it back to his parking spot, it's gone too. He circles the block three times until he gives up and double-parks and waits for another hour before his wife shows up.

Why the bloody hell did you stay away so long? he grumbles.

It took me quite a while to find a shelter that had enough room for both the kids and me. But we can't move in until Monday.

Great. He notices just then that she looks a little draggy.

It's the street or back to the boyfriend, she pouts, which used to look very good on her when she was much younger and without a black eye. When he says nothing, she says to the children: Where did you put your coats? They start quarreling, the dog gains purchase on one of his mikes with its teeth and after he rescues it, he sighs Okay.

Her face brightens. Just for the weekend.

I have to sleep in the van anyway. Here are the apartment keys. Make sure the dog gets walked.

My boy will do it. He thinks it's his dog.

He knows that's a threat. Great, he says. Now get out of here.

Chapter 26

I LAND as light as a leaf on a car hood on top of the parking structure. But not light enough—the alarm goes off. It's landing that harpies have to learn, not flying, and I am never going to master the Peter Pan drop. But since I'm always late, hardly anyone's around. I trudge over to the elevator, fooling with my key fob to suggest I'm trying to turn off the alarm in case anybody notices.

Not a soul, thank god.

Stewie's waiting for me in reserved parking three flights down, standing beside our van in his hoodie as always, even though it's already quite warm.

Are you putting out some kind of a political statement, I say, tugging at the hood. It'll be close to eighty today.

Like the hoodie makes me more of a target? All politics aside, I am *in* my hood when I wear it, I am present and witnessing. But look who's talking—what about that ratty jacket you're always stuffed into?

I bridle at his accuracy. All my straining at the seams has begun to show and the jacket's starting to fall apart. I have to get to a tailor. I get cold sometimes, I tell him. I wrap the jacket tighter. Especially when I'm talking to clients. They scare me.

They do not, he says, laughing. I've never seen you scared about anything. You just think you look cute.

I puff up and strut my two steps over to the passenger side. You and me—put together we're like cookies and milk, I say, opening the door.

Mac and cheese, he says, laughing again.

Chips and salsa.

I do a little shuffle. Salt and vinegar.

Strawberries and cream. Too good, he says, swinging into his seat.

Rum and coke?

You win. We high-five.

I really need this kind of approval. I'm nervous, twitchy, the way I always am after a smote.

You know, says Stewie after I'm seatbelted, you're great, and we're partners and everything, but I'm very fond of your friend Roxy. I made a play for her a while ago, but I don't think she even noticed.

Stewie.

He's looking out the windshield. Whatever it is that Tim's got jinxes me every which way.

You're shy, I say.

Not very. It's Roxy. She's too involved with him to look at anybody else, he says, pulling out of the parking lot.

I agree but I don't say anything. The last thing I want is another human tempting her.

Stewie deals with the traffic.

Beneath his tough exterior lies a heart too soft for this work. I mean, look at his patience, the way he sees all sides to a situation. I sure wish he were the candidate in question rather than Tim. I do wonder about his knowing the color of skin under a bird's wing, the ever-present hoodie for wing hiding, his love of kale—but social workers do tend toward the eccentric, given that their job is so stressful. But if he showed up at one of our occasional harpy gettogethers, well, I wouldn't be totally surprised. It's not as if I can call a meeting just to check his identity—or I would've checked Tim's a long time ago. Harpies aren't going to take time off to fly in for just a head count. You need a big celebration or a real emergency to call a gathering. Even so, not all the harpies come to these parties, though they will always try, since they're so infrequent and we're so few now. It's too dangerous for everyone to be caught together.

But I can dream. For invitations, we pluck out what appears to be an ordinary chicken feather from a particular place on our shoulders—feathers anybody with harpy vision can see in a color humans can't. The feathers can even be spotted from the sky. We scatter them around harpy-type places, groves of any kind of nut, remote vistas, nesting nooks, then everyone congregates in the nearest hideout: best a crevasse or a cave where no one can find us—no satellites, no drones. For drink, we bring whatever noxious liquor the era has a fondness for, and loop around in the night air, claws out. I remember some of the older ones pushing fermented berries on the younger ones. We have a water mister that everyone loves. We like to fly-race to practice our flapping power so we could be good, very good, at plucking prey out of the sky. And other things. You've seen the surfing swans with a million other YouTube viewers? Or birds rolling down the snowy hood of a car? People like to think that's all the enjoyment birds get because it's something humans would do, but would they recognize a species at play if it weren't like theirs? Every seemingly tame harpy in the world goes wild at our parties, even the elders, who are practically clawless. It's our one chance to acknowledge the love of our species and how much humans keep us apart, and the only time we can see the faces of male harpies. But even the remotest sites are starting to degrade now, with water even deer avoid, a plethora of overbearing insects in the bark of the trees—if not the air—and wily mold invasions.

This is not an emergency.

A couple of days later, Chris is smacking a new skateboard to the pavement with some other kids in front of the social services building. A present from Dad, he says, swiping past me. Shades cover his face to conceal the scratches around his eyes from the accident, so he looks very cool. The other skaters whip their boards past him and each other with such serious faces you'd think they foresaw their own injuries, or at least their teeth falling out on impact. Who knows what Chris has told them about his face, what wild story he made up involving the skateboard. Stewie mentioned the other day how he ended his own skateboarding career with a spectacular smashup. He even pulled up his cuffs so I could see the scar on his ankle where they sewed him up, and then he identified each capped tooth. Chris's face is just as serious but also a little dull—the new medication. We have a new windshield too, he says.

I nod and wait for the other kids to wander off—Evacuate! Adult in the vicinity!—I say Hey, as soon as they disappear. Why have I never seen your mother?

Okay, so maybe that's not the most politic thing to ask a guy who's just out of the hospital from a breakdown, but I want to get to the bottom of this. And, yes, clients are supposed to volunteer information if they want us to know anything that's not in their file.

Chris skates back and forth on the sidewalk, each time a little faster.

It was his mom who alerted social services in the first place, according to what records I could find, and now she's out of the picture entirely? I get in the way again to slow him down, I stand in his path and wave my hands, but he shears around me with his board, he bangs right into my shin the next time.

The river, he says. You have to forget.

I pretend to swim that river. He pretends to pop a couple of pills.

One solution. I nod in complete agreement.

He flips his board around. You said you'd get me that buckle.

Yeah, I did. So?

So where is it? He smacks his board up, he smacks it down.

Okay, okay, I say, stay here.

I go back into the office and find what I ordered online two weeks ago at the back of my locker.

He's swinging the end of his board around with his foot when I get back, looking surprised by my quick return.

It's yours, I say. How are you going to attach it?

He turns the buckle over in his hand. There's the sharp part that you pound around the end of the leather, he says. You need to hit it good and hard with a hammer. You need to pound it even along both sides. He pockets it and skate-boards furiously up the sidewalk, barely avoiding two kids carrying their boards to the park, he skates back and forth on the board in a trance.

I rub where he bruised my shin and watch him. He's smiling. Look at that—I made a kid happy—and I didn't have to kill anybody to do it!

Someone new shows up with a broken board, and more kids come out of the woodwork to crowd around him with advice, even our own security guard. Chris skates back over to me.

What?

He holds out the buckle. You wouldn't give this to me if you were my mother. It could be dangerous.

How?

They take belts and shoelaces away from mental patients.

He's daring me.

Keep it, I say.

Icarus is the emblem of the bipolar. Fly up as high as you can go, then drop. The full story is that the king of Crete ordered a maze built to imprison the Minotaur (half-bull, half-man, another outlier in the gene pool) and Icarus's dad was the carpenter. When the Cretan princess and her boyfriend found and killed the Minotaur, the king felt betrayed by shoddy workmanship and imprisoned Icarus's father inside the maze. Icarus must have been his father's assistant, and so suffered the same punishment. After waiting around for geese and whatever else on their flight path to drop their feathers, and then melting all the candles they could find, he and his father crafted waxy feathered lift-off gear for them both. The point of the story is supposed to be about hubris, a kid getting too big for his britches and flying too high, but you have to cut him some slack. First of all, consider that the boy had more muscles than his dad and of course would go higher, and of course would want to, after being cooped up in a maze for so long. Really, it's a story about a boy who needs to go high to feel alive but he's at the whim of gravity on the way down. Bipolar. The feat had other names for a millennium—*wild, wrong.*

I don't tell Chris about Icarus.

Chapter 27

ON MONDAY, Robinson visits the apartment for a change of clothes. With her, it's never just a few days at his place. The kids are still asleep and his wife is making herself coffee. He stumbles through the toys and food wrappers and socks and an egg-yolk-covered bib thrown to the floor. Some of the rest is swept to the side and some of it is picked up and draped on the furniture. Deep in a dresser drawer in the bedroom he finds socks and T-shirts. He keeps his clothes in drawers, why can't they? Okay, they don't have drawers here anymore but that was his first question to his wife when they got together and she agreed, but the clothes were never put away. It wasn't solely her job to pick them up, no, it wasn't only a woman's work. Not that her selling cigarettes out of a tiny booth on a busy thoroughfare was so much women's work either but there you go, she said, that's what happens when you major in English. Marriage is something two people do, she said. Pitch in.

He said Clinton and Obama turned out all right with single parents.

Why did I marry you? was how she answered that one.

Because I had the better job, he thinks now. Or is it because he likes to tell the kids jokes—what a great audience!—and pretend to wrestle with the oldest and treat the middle girl with a chocolate donut once in a while.

He showers, and it surprises him that he likes hearing the kids shrieking and babbling in the other room while she gets them ready for school. They're a lot better company now that they're older. Or at least they don't annoy him the way they used to. One of them comes in with a press-on eagle tattoo and he even lets the kid stick it on the back of his neck. Looks great, says the kid, his smile a few teeth short.

He can't see the tattoo himself.

While he screws on his socks in the living room, his wife says, Do you think a shelter's like a hotel I just check into?

He ties his shoes. You kids, he says, want to go to a fun fair with me this weekend? I read about it online. The dog will love it, lots of crazy birds. We could go as a family. And I could take pictures of everybody with my new lens.

Oh, Robinson, she says, you're so sentimental.

Don't get any ideas, he says.

Chapter 28

ROXY TAKES a long time polishing her nails. A modest rose, not the bloody red red. I can barely smell the garbage on the street over the nail polish, and just a whiff of the blooming early honeysuckle on the back fence. It's Friday night and there's a light warm breeze from the window brushing my feathers.

When I went into Tim's office yesterday, I say, he was leaning out the window just the way I would. You know, a little too far.

He likes to go too far. She flaps her fingers to make the paint dry. Just like you.

Maybe there *is* something birdy about him, I may have misjudged him.

She stops blowing on her nails. Don't tease me. You convinced me that he wasn't harpy after he didn't eat the fish on that ferry trip. How could he turn down a live fish? You think I'm never listening to you, but I am. It takes me a while to process. He's just another blotto human, dumb to like me.

I'm sorry, I say. And I am. I hate to see her so sad. But if she's really giving him up, yippee, I can move on. I don't pressure her though because she could be saying things like that just to get rid of me, regretful she made the call—let her prove it.

Saturday we sign up for a conservationist project to clean up a woodland trail. Lots of unruly foliage and nest bits, a kind of *Call of the Wild* for us, where we can stand still and enjoy looking up through the branches and nobody shoots us for trespassing. So what if I have a little too much fun and eat termites from the tree base—nobody catches me.

The conservation people serve coffee and give out free bird whistles. The lead person demonstrates whistling as if she invented it and talks about how in Bhutan it came in so handy. She is exceptionally long-necked, quite a specimen herself, but she doesn't know the whistle needs two tones, not three, and keeps staring at Roxy. Apparently the woman's hosting the grand opening of a gigantic aviary in a week after some kind of festive bird fair in the area. She even gives out brochures.

Roxy doesn't dwell too long on her sadness with regard to Tim, which is either a relief or suspicious. I can't decide. The next morning, she hops right out of bed to scan her email. We should do something really special before you leave. She clacks her bright nails against the keys. What about making a trip to the Ye Olde Bird Fair that woman mentioned?

I stare at the colorful tents on the website, the happy crowds. I say, I'm not going to leave until I'm totally sure.

You really don't believe me? She claps her wings together. I'm over him. Totally.

Think of it this way—I could fly off and he'd be at you in a minute. Game over.

Okay, okay, she sighs, be paranoid. This bird fair thing isn't too far away.

I didn't know there was such a thing. Sounds downright British. They certainly don't do things like that in France.

A tristate event, she reads from the screen. Once every five years, it says here.

I start looking around for my shoes and jacket. Maybe she's right, I should ditch her, leave her to her fate, and get out before anything develops on the negative side vis-à-vis the missing Collinses.

About five thousand bird nuts are pouring in through the gate by the time we drive up. My sister read that the event was going to be big, but I hadn't expected huge. Mobile vendors add to the chaos, selling souvenir wings and various light-up bird trash throughout the crowd. It's a real extravaganza, she says, gesturing toward the twelve-foot-tall wooden parrot, wings extended over the gate, the regal hawk and an ostrich supporting it.

It must have been hard to pick mascots that didn't eat each other, I say, as we fight our way to the ticket booth, jostled by a group of too-enthusiastic birders.

She whistles low, using the one the conservationist handed out. Nobody notices. They're all doing something similar, showing off their own bird prowess, tit callers, screeches, half in the costume of the birdwatcher, the other half looking and sounding birdy. Surely someone here is a harpy. It used to be easy to tell: the humped, the beaked, the limping, but since we've really perfected our humanness, we'd probably need a costume.

We join a new line to get wristbands and are just about through it when I spot Tim already inside. Does his being here confirm that he's harpy? I don't say anything so tantalizing to Roxy, hoping somehow to avoid him altogether, but he ambushes us as soon as we're banded.

Just as a friend, Roxy swears as he approaches.

Of course she texted him with an invite. You've seen the parrots already? I point at one of his fingers wrapped in gauze. Puts a spin on the term *hand-fed*.

I must have looked a little too pleased at his being wounded because he says, It probably won't even get infected and fall off.

We go on like this as if we are actually friends at work, but soon my tune changes. Even walking on the other side of Roxy, I can smell his scent. It's intoxicating. Roxy is right—I do get confused between being a concerned sister and an interested party. Mix all this with how disappointed

I am with Roxy's fickleness, how trashed I feel about that. It took her about five seconds to change her mind. Why can't she stick to her resolve and ditch him?

Where have you been since the picnic? I ask since my sister won't.

You see me every day at work.

That's not what Coco means, says my sister, rolling her eyes, affirming in full the revival of her interest.

We hit the fair's big top just then, where it's hard for Roxy to stay quite so obsessed. Along with birding equipment and the clothes to stalk them in, there are bird-watching vacations and booths on camping with birds beside booths with live maggots for sale, six varieties of suet, a hundred mix-it-yourself samples of exotic birdseed, not to mention birdie basketball, a Supreme Cotton Tail Preening Toy, Sleepy Teepees, and something called a Reinforcing Foraging Wheel.

I thought the bird salespeople would all be old men with advanced degrees tutting over pedigrees or overweight middle-aged spinsters in polka-dotted dresses displaying canaries in a cage. Instead, bikers with hairdos that match the cockatoos on their shoulders stroll around with price tags on the birds' claws, booth babes in bikinis sell veritable flocks of giant inflatable birds and bird flags, and one tiny young woman holds a hooded falcon nearly her size. This has nothing to do with Tim being intoxicating, the whole place is just plain thrilling from a bird's point of view. Well, and human, since the sleaze factor is pretty high. Cockfighting isn't advertised but every so often some-body walks by fingering a bright green ticket with a dollar amount printed on the side. Birds are killing each other somewhere for human profit.

At our first booth stop, Roxy asks Tim to throw darts to win a live chick for her, a cute bundle of yellow fluff that makes at least me really hungry.

While Tim fails to hit the target, I spot the woman with all the holes in the walls, still with her whiskery pony-tail, but wearing pretend chicken feet and standing next to, of all people, Robinson, who's restraining his dog. He's wearing a vest but the rest of his torso's bare, with a camera and its ridiculous lens front and center, and a tattoo of the wings of an eagle across the back of his neck. A guy that size should stay fully clothed is my first thought, it's certainly no disguise. The dog's one of those hunting types and is a nervous wreck, given the circumstances. I give Robinson my usual cheerful hi while his dog snaps at me, and then one to her as if we were cordial, as if I hadn't just come to collect her kids a few days ago like dry cleaning she'd left at the door. I'm happy that the bat guy is not with her—but Robinson? I take a second look while he snaps a picture of the three kids dressed like chicks standing in front of the woman. He just doesn't strike me as the fatherly type. The woman splits with two of the kids right after he takes the picture, heading toward the big top, and he's left with the youngest and the dog. Does that mean they aren't together, or they just don't get along?

I say nothing about them to Tim and Roxy who've given up winning chicks. Not their business. Then we pass rescue birds in cages every few feet. It is ironic that the two of us are not avian enough to prefer rescuing birds over children, but the damaged baby birds do evoke my pity. It's kind of like lactation in mammals, I think, a tingling in the wings. With that and getting claustrophobic because Tim is so close, and Robinson's surveilling not such a discrete distance behind us with the little girl trailing him, crying because he can't find cotton candy to buy, my wings flex hard against my jacket. Excuse me, I say to my sister and Tim. I'm off to the Ladies'.

I release my wings in the stall. Someone waiting asks where I found a bird with those colors, and I realize I'm molting again. It has to be because of proximity to Tim. Then I see chicken feet in the stall beside me and I panic. Is she following me too? I dislike coincidence, I'm afraid of it. Ladies line the space in front of the stalls, there's only one door out. I could just stuff my wings back into my jacket and push through the line to the door but the skylight tempts me—it's so much faster. Can I still wing it straight up? No one will see me after I pop this little distractor: the live rat in my pocket, lunch. As quick as it scurries out under the stall, the screaming begins.

My sister and Tim have wandered away—or else he's taken her away, confirming the worst of my fears. This whole pas de deux thing can't go on much longer. I text her. No answer. I visit the nearby tents: Mouth-to-Beak Resuscitation, Cleaning the Cloaca, Birds: The Wilder the Better. No sister. Good thing nobody thinks my losing a few feathers is weird in this group, which is what is happening as a result of ripping my jacket on the skylight. What a mess! I'm not as accurate a flyer as I used to be and hit the hardware a little off-center. I keep my arm clamped to my side and stick my head into the next tent. It's the Condor Act: a snake, twisted into a pretzel around a post to avoid the big bird that's hunched low, intent, clasped at the feet by its trainer. The audience—every one of them likewise mesmerized—press in on both sides, all of them craning. The room is dark, hot, fetid, smelling of snake and bird and whatever treat the bird is going to get besides the snake. Just as I'm trying to make out who's who, the trainer, a guy smoking a fat cigar, releases the condor.

For a few seconds, it seems as if the snake is going to win.

I catch my sister across the booth, cheering, and Tim so close to her, watching the bird, fear tight across his face.

Chapter 29

ON MONDAY, about ten minutes after Tim gets to the office, a cop and a big lady lieutenant in a too-tight uniform come to call, wanting to know if the agency had somebody with a key to the Collinses' place.

They were parents of a kid under your care, right? says the lieutenant.

What rookies. His people don't have keys, he told them. They have to knock. What's the problem with the Collinses?

Missing now about ten days.

Usually those types come back from their vacation as soon as their money runs out.

Is this their case worker? The lieutenant shows Coco's photo to Tim, something from maybe high school, she looks so young.

Tim's heart rate goes up. Judge-appointed, he says. Can't do better than that. Nice girl, he says, though that sort of sticks in his craw.

We'd like to talk to her.

He pauses. I'll let her know.

The lieutenant lifts an eyebrow, but then she nods as if what he said made all the difference and leaves a card.

He doesn't trust them, and he certainly doesn't like getting so close, chatting them up as if he were some kind of buddy. It reminds him of all those times he almost did get arrested. He'll ask Coco if she knows anything more about the Collinses, but she sure doesn't like to take questions from him. Should he even mention the cops to her? Roxy acted a little weird at the fair, wouldn't leave Coco and go home with him.

He should've been more aggressive. He rubs at the back of his neck.

At least they only want Coco.

Tim needs a drink after the cop visit. Or two. He's glad when Reagan telephones for a meeting, especially when she suggests a place that is not her Club, but he waits practically twenty minutes outside the Birdcage for her to get out of her car. Finally she waves at him to go inside—and then proceeds to talk another ten minutes. Someone from Malaysia wants the egg of a gray parrot, she says as soon as she takes a seat at the bar. They're crazy about grays. As soon as anything gets labeled endangered, the birds had better start laying, and I don't mean for themselves.

Tim has already finished his first drink. Every five seconds the various parrots in elaborate cages in front of the bar shriek out *Gimme a kiss* and *I'm going to get you*. Reagan doesn't seem to mind; she smiles every time they scream. The bartender, dolled up in a skimpy feather costume, takes her time putting a cover over the loudest one, and only then pulls out an order pad and asks him for his refill: Grey Goose, Rooster Tail, Wild Turkey, or Jungle Bird?

This themed stuff gets old. What's in that last one? Something to kill the parrot?

Aren't you a wise guy? says the bartender. Look, I'll take the cover off and you can discuss it.

Not to bother, he says. A Grey Goose.

A Goose for me too, says Reagan. She's without décolleté, no sidelong glances, no Honey-would-you-do-this-for-me. The aviary is finished, she says, as soon as the bartender goes about her business. The idea now is to get the bird to me without a lot of fuss, right? Soon?

He could laugh at how easy she makes that sound. Then he does laugh, and a bird starts imitating him, and he laughs again. The mirror behind it makes it funnier. The bartender sets down their drinks.

She leans toward him. You know, it's not like she's going to mate with you for life.

Did you arrange this meeting just to tell me that?

You can get out at any time, she says, putting the same purse that held the gun between them. Just no balance on what I owe you if you don't complete the job. I'll hire someone else. In fact, I know someone who's available right now.

She's staring into the mirror, at herself, her hands beside

her drink. He's sure she's bluffing. I thought the job was over after I watched her and took notes, he says, but then you said I had to produce the DNA, and then you said physical proof, and then you said I had to make her fall in love with me.

I never said anything about love, she says. Just turn her over. As simple as that. She points at one of the birds. See how much that parrot's fussing? It's getting ready to lay.

The parrot squawks.

He signals the bartender for the check, then drinks down the liquor and plays with what's left of his ice cubes with the cocktail stick. He's not so concerned about the money, he's more afraid that whomever she gets to replace him will fool with Roxy. Maybe hurt her. I can always make a living in social services, he says, not without sarcasm.

Free vocational training, she says. She nibbles at the cherry skewered over her ice. Have any of the parents of your clients disappeared?

Yeah, he says. What do you know about that?

That might be due to a certain employee in your work-force, she says into the mirror. Harpies can be very danger-ous. Best you get the job over with.

In what way dangerous? I mean, there's a lot of legends about them, a couple of video games, but really—danger-ous? A bird? He straightens up, he's a little loud, and the parrots are getting riled up. She doesn't seem so bad to me.

They have a temper, these birds. You don't want to cross them. I imagine that a truly difficult situation would set her off. Have you ever seen what an eagle can do with a lamb?

He remembers the condor. Reagan has a cruel mouth that's very precisely lipsticked bright red; it looks as if she's bleeding around her teeth. I imagine you could have caught her a dozen times so far, she's saying. What's stopping you?

The bartender arrives with the check.

He's not going to let her intimidate him, he's not going to tell the bitch he could have abducted Roxy easily with her friend gone somewhere at the bird fair, but he was filled with so much fear and lust and so conflicted he couldn't lift a finger. What the hell? he says. I know what I'm doing. I just need a little more time, and another decent advance.

She frowns at the parrots in the mirror and lets out the quietest of laughs. Nothing substantial has been accomplished yet, why should I pay you another cent? Just get the bird and don't antagonize it.

He grabs the vial out of his coat pocket and holds it out to her. Well, I've had enough of this stuff.

Getting bird-on-the-brain? Tough guy like you? She laughs and pushes the vial back into his hand. Take it—it gives you superpowers.

Chapter 30

I LIKE the 5 p.m. to 1 a.m. shift in social services better than the days—all the kids are home, you don't have to visit the schools, and you're on if the parents decide to turn the kids in for good. I'm not too excited about the last but it's a long way from the twelfth century when they drowned them in a sack under cover of darkness. Stewie prefers this shift too, when he can get it, since he can nap in the van.

The mall beside the office where we park is faux colonial: white pillars, wrought-iron detail, bay windows, and cupolas. That colonial era was not my favorite. I was flying around West Africa then, trying to hide children from the thugs in Portugal who, being from a small nation, needed a lot of slaves to make it bigger. One day I was blown way off-course and ended up in the rockiest part of Massachusetts. After spooking the Wampanoag the first night with my feather drying, I "liberated"—isn't that the term humans used for stealing in the 1970s?—a deerskin outfit and crashed the Thanksgiving feast the next day. The four

Pilgrim wives who survived the crossing had to feed over a hundred guests at the first three-day feast. They didn't care what I was dressed in, they were grateful for my help.

You might say I came over with the Mayflower.

Stewie's sound asleep when the police call around midnight to tell us to come down to the station to pick somebody up, there's no parent answering his call. Who is it? I ask, but they've already hung up.

The cop at the front is keeping the kid locked in a cell—he tried to run even after they cuffed him. The cop wants him arraigned in the morning and sent off to a ranch. You know the kind of ranch I mean? he says to me. We had to send in a copter to get him and the rest of the kids. It's expensive.

Stewie's still rubbing his face awake.

A second cop in the holding area gives us the rest of the story. It turns out that six kids were hanging out in the park late, after curfew—You're enforcing it? I say to the officer, and he shrugs—when one cop, well, a couple or more, decide to approach, to find out what's going on. Seeing them advancing with their guns out, the boys fled deeper into the park, they ran in different directions. We had to put out a call, maybe it's a gang up to no good, says the officer. You know? The helicopter got to be part of that, and it worked out because we got to use our new gear and heat-sense the leader out of a compost pile. He could've smothered and died, says the cop. We got them all, and all the other parents have already put up bail except for this one.

Maybe he'll learn a lesson about staying out so late, says the front officer, handing the other cop a piece of paper. His pop doesn't keep his phone on. The kid gave us your number.

Chris is pacing his cell like he's high, but kids his age have this great energy whether they're high or stressed or not. Maybe he's screwed up again and hasn't taken his meds. It's not as if he looks happy to see us. I wasn't even with those guys, they weren't even my friends is the first thing he says.

Just leave him here, says Stewie, disgusted by his whining.

I don't think so, I say, stepping closer. I think there's more to this. He ought to be freaked that his dad's not coming. As soon as he passes me again, I grab him through the bars by his new buckle.

He shrieks.

Where's your dad?

Coco, warns Stewie.

I pull Chris to my face. I sniff. You smell like the shit you hid in. Then I release him, and he stumbles backward.

Behind me the cop says, You're his social worker?

Cool off, says Stewie. We'll sign for him, he says to the cop. My signature's on file.

The cop sizes him up. Stewie makes the sign *What?* with his hands. Here's my ID.

Okay, the cop says to Chris. Go on. He unlocks the cell. They'll take you home.

Now the boy doesn't want to leave, he doesn't want to come with us. He's upset. He shakes his head.

Stewie says in a steady, neutral voice: What's the problem, Chris?

Slowly the kid raises his hands to the front of his face so we can't see the sob start.

What Chris needs, I say to Stewie as we drive him home, is somebody full-time to keep him out of trouble, someone very patient.

A guardian angel, says Stewie. Chris has fallen asleep in the back seat.

Yeah, well, what would compel an angel—if they really exist—to guard children 24/7? The wrath of god? Or is guard duty one way to pay for the privilege of having wings? Or is it the usual Judeo-Christian mean-spirited father figure making sure he has no rivals in the angels by keeping them busy with kids? Angels are a projection by children who don't believe the amorphous god to be everywhere but instead imagine a sort of dog, only with wings instead of wag, that follows them around. Or else an angel is a sop for a parent who doesn't have time to hover over the child himself.

Where is Chris's father? asks Stewie.

Just drop me off, I'll manage, Chris starts in as soon as we stop. He's wired. It's as if his little nap was eight hours long. You can't get in anyway, don't bother, it's locked up. I'll go in through a window.

It won't look good for you or for us if you end up at the

station again. I keep a grip on him while Stewie locates a
spare key behind the overflowing mailbox. We climb the
three flights with Chris in reluctant lead, unlock the door,
and find his father lying across the floor of the living room,
unconscious.

His pulse is faint and Stewie phones for an ambulance.

He's not drunk, he says after sniffing him. Was there a
break-in and your dad surprised the guy? What exactly happened?

Chris just stands there.

Stewie's not only one of the kids when they're in trouble,
he's also a surrogate for every kid's parent, and so this is an
attack on him. He starts pacing the room.

Did you put him out and then run into the park? he
asks.

Chris stays silent.

I bend down to check on his father myself; he's barely
breathing. That's when Stewie catches Chris with a lamp
in his hand, trying to bean me. He grabs his wrist. The kid
starts yelling I don't know what, there's so much profanity.

We have to get him to a shrink again, says Stewie, soon.
He peels the neck of the lamp out of Chris' grip. To the
lock-up first, then a shrink.

No, he screams. No, no. He manages to hit Stewie pretty
hard in the belly with his loose fist. Stewie gasps.

I grab Chris, grip both his wrists together, and make the
call one-handed.

Hey, if that's Roxy you're calling, she's senior, says Stewie.

We're in deep shit if she shows up. The ambulance will be here soon enough.

Chris whimpers.

Roxy can sign the consent form, not us, I say. We don't want Tim here. We glare at each other while I give my sister the address. I need some help, I tell her.

While we wait, Stewie drags the kid into a more comfortable position on the sofa where I can sit and wedge Chris's hands into mine and my grip won't hurt him so much. The kid ends up leaning his head against mine. I stroke his hair and he doesn't flinch.

Don't you love your father? Stewie asks. He's the only one you've got.

Chris mutters, won't answer.

Stewie opens all the cabinets in the bathroom and then the drawers in Chris's room as if someone's hiding somewhere, or he's trying to figure out what happened. I hiss, Evidence! Leave it!

The father groans at last, and Stewie gives up his wandering and tends to him. Chris stiffens in my arms, worrying with his body. I hear my sister at the window in the next room, a mistake since we're three flights up. Despite knowing this is not a good thing, I lash the kid to the furniture with the lamp cord and help her in.

I didn't want to make a lot of noise, knocking, she whispers as she climbs in from the fire escape. Might be trouble.

I give her the "you idiot" look.

Stewie's still bent over the father in the front room when

Roxy enters. Glad you could make it, he says, and frowns at the wrist he's holding. Pulse still not good.

You're Chris? she says to the boy who's in my grip again, then she kneels and touches his father's temple, pulls open his eyelids. No drugs. Hit on the head?

Maybe, says Stewie. I think he's been out an awfully long time.

Sirens are making their noise up the street. Just let me have the form and I'll sign it, she says.

Right, he says again, and finds the paper.

She signs and is turning into the next room just as the ambulance pulls up. We'll sort out the rest of this tomorrow.

Hey, says Stewie, the front door's the other way.

When the father finally comes to, he doesn't remember what happened, so the medics have to be sure his collapse isn't something to do with his brain. The hospital will keep him overnight, I explain to Chris. It would be better for Chris and his father's health if his father remembered he had been hit on the head, rather than have to assume he blacked out and fell down. While Emergency works on him, the shrink on call glances at the form and gives Chris a sedative and says he should go home.

You'll feel better soon, I tell Chris.

He's plugged his ears.

I confer with my sister on the phone. He might flip out, I say. I'm taking him with us.

makes his way over to the flashlights and the tape around the two bodies. The lady lieutenant from before waves him over.

Somebody running along the road caught a big whiff of them, she says.

Tim turns and vomits while the Emergency workers behind him bag what's left. The lieutenant's sidekick is taking pictures.

They weren't the cleanest couple, she says, inputting data on her device with one well-manicured finger. Dope and pills on them.

Suicide? he says, feeling suddenly very sober.

I don't know. They fell from a height but the bridge and anything else high enough for this kind of damage is a long way from here. She leans back into her leather: the belt, the holster. Maybe they were killed as a warning to other dealers. We found a pen with your organization's name on it.

Thieves, too.

She looks past the bodies with her flashlight, toward the dark tufts of grass four feet further, and he looks there too as if they held the answer. She snaps her device closed. I've talked with someone who has a wild idea. There were these weird suicides/homicides in France too, somebody falling from high up in not quite the right place. Interpol sent a memo around months ago, and we had a good laugh about it. I'll send you the details in case you can help. And we'll have to have a talk with the employee involved in the case.

Tim nods, gripping his hands tight behind his back. I'm happy to do what I can, but I don't see what this has to do with us—or really, how I can help.

You never know. The lieutenant stuffs the device back into her equipment belt. Thank god for this new database. It covers all through Europe, even Asia, and now here. Sure you don't have any ideas? We've checked you out. Sure you're really in social work?

Hey—he says, lighten up. I've always been in social work.

The lieutenant chuckles. Okay, she says. Stay out of trouble.

On his way back to his car, he's brushing another damn bird off his shoulder when it occurs to him that birds don't sing in the dark, what are they doing singing?

Chapter 32

YOU CAN stay the night as long as you take the bus to the shrink's in the morning by yourself, I tell Chris. I'll meet you there afterward and bring you to your dad at the hospital. That's the deal. I have to punch in at work.

You trust me to take the bus by myself?

He's distracted by Roxy who's coming out of the bedroom in her pj's, the ones with glittery stripes.

Yeah, Mr. Tough Guy, I say. I don't tell him the medication should make him much calmer.

He finds a tennis ball under the couch and bounces it in every corner of the apartment. Cool, he says when it hits the bedroom door and Roxy's sparkly junk starts escaping—rhinestone-covered beer openers, matted tinsel, three gold hoops. After taking apart most of an old bird-armed turntable that Roxy someday intends to spray silver, Chris finally starts to nod off, then barely manages to make it to the couch to collapse.

I sit in front of the door under a blanket in the dark,

keeping an eye on him. Who knows how long he'll sleep this time?

Roxy flops down on the chair across from the couch. Other than Mom, she whispers, what do you think makes us so defensive about kids?

It's not like this is the first time you've asked that. I curl into my blanket. The thing with instinct, it's unconscious.

Unconscious like—I was asleep at the time? My sister uses her druggy voice. Usually you bring up that Adam and Eve story about harpies being born from the blood of some god's castration by his father. Revenge on the parent.

I'm so over myth. Maybe it's all because we reenact that trauma of getting pushed out of the nest every time we step off the sill.

All birds get pushed out of the nest, she says. I love flying. She covers her eyes and sighs. If humans died out, we'd rejoice and inherit the world.

I laugh but not ha-ha. Snatchers, that's what the Greeks used to call us.

They were so busy inventing proto-computers, looking at the stars, plundering and conquering that they were never very good at watching kids. She sips a glass of water. Do you actually want to stop?

I pull the covers around me a little tighter. I can stop.

I did, says Roxy. Why I haven't—

The boy turns over.

This one's not abused, I say. I just have that feeling. That's why we're keeping him here and not turning him in. We've had kids like this before. They straighten out with the right diagnosis.

Wait a minute, says my sister. He's going home as soon as he can.

Right, right, I tell her, raising my crossed fingers.

She leans from her chair and, with one hand, covers the boy a little better with his blanket, but that disturbs him and he sits up, his eyes filled with wildness. Dad?

Nobody knows what's wrong with him yet, says my sister. You might as well get more sleep. It's way late.

We're quiet quiet quiet while he looks around. The streetlight shows his eyes wide and unfocused. Want some hot chocolate? I say. I don't think that's contraindicated with what they gave you. I should have thought of that sooner.

I hate chocolate, he says, blinking slowly.

Hard to believe, I say as his hand creeps over the side of the couch toward his sneakers. Where do you think you're going?

He drops the shoe he's grabbed and lurches barefoot toward the door. I changed my mind, he shouts, let me out of here. He fumbles at the knob.

Both of us clasp him on the shoulders and press him back into the couch. So much for the sleeping pill, I say. It's only one night, I tell him.

His eyes dart, he avoids ours. I knew all along you guys were weird.

Aha, the boy has ears, I say.

Relax, Roxy says. It's for your own good, she says, leaning close to him.

What about Adam and Eve and snatchers and what is it that you want to stop doing? His muscles bunch and resist but we don't answer. There's no moving anywhere with the two of us pinning him down, staring hard at him and his every twitch, and he starts mumbling about his rights, his rights, about how the two of us talk so much alike, and what about his rights? But then the drug wells up, there's a sudden drop in resistance, he relaxes fully and closes his eyes.

Chapter 33

THE NEIGHBORHOOD'S now got a double defenestration on the books, the news according to Robinson's police scanner. Not so different from what's described in the warrant he was given from Europe. When he inquires, the office tells him not to worry, this investigation's being handled solely by local enforcement, not them. They don't want to attract attention by intervening—yet. Just keep shooting, they tell him. You bought a new lens—use it. They expect to see the whole kit and caboodle this time.

He reads the warrant a little more carefully. Over thirty murders—or suicides?—bodies falling from high places all over Europe and no one ever sees the victims climbing to the roof of tall buildings or checking out cliffs? Enforcement wouldn't have strung them together if it hadn't been for the demise of the French prime minister's nephew. He died from a fall in Paris, but too far from the Eiffel Tower to make sense, holding a steel box full of documents about his being part of an underage sex ring.

Seems like she did the French a favor. But she must be amazingly strong to lift a struggling man holding a heavy box.

The report lists her as a flight risk.

She's always a flight risk, if what he recorded last week is any indication. Of course, he's going to rerecord. Nobody will believe what he has. He doesn't believe it himself. Maybe there's a defect in the lens, an augmented reality thing. Whatever.

Could be dangerous, says the warrant.

Could be an understatement.

He googles mightily with what little information he has, and prints pictures of the victims and a map to show where they were found, just the way they do in the movies. He tapes the printouts to his corkboard beside the monitor and finds little plastic tacks and rubber bands to connect one victim to another. If only he can figure out what connects them in real life, then he can predict when she'll strike next. He stares at the corkboard, rubber bands in hand. The case is warming up. He just has to decide whether to send in that really weird footage. Flying out of the top of the women's bathroom? Or maybe he should just order a straitjacket and be done with it. Surveillo-phrenic they call it, what you get when you spend too much time doing this kind of work.

He needs a motive. And inspiration. He looks around the messy dash, the cupholder, the crumpled napkins.

Where's his coffee? He hates it when Coco works all night. He has to stay all jazzed up. He seldom shadows her at work these days. She has to behave there anyway is what he's decided, so that's when he rests. Or calls the kids to see if they want to talk to him. They are still excited about that bird fair. But right now they're asleep. He goes for a playlist that starts with the Beatles' "It Won't Be Long" to keep himself awake. The dog climbs into his lap. Big for that, even in the La-Z-Boy, but they manage, although the dog insists on thoroughly cleaning his face with his tongue. How can he do surveillance while he's being bathed? Where are last night's tapes? He means to get around to them, but he has the dog to walk and he has to check on the van's tires. Can't be too safe. He's pretty safe in his chair. He nods off.

The dog stiffens in his lap, lunges for the door. Relax, he mutters. Coco's driven up.

In the half dark under the flickering street light that illuminates the weird angle he has on her door, Coco leaves the car with someone short. A date? As soon as she's inside, he scans the net for short people: Tom Cruise, five seven; Danny Devito, four ten; Genghis Khan, five one; Houdini, five four.

What's he doing? He's not on the celebrity shift anymore. He finds his coffee. Reviewing the tape again, he decides it's a kid, tall for his age, and she's pushing him inside. Why didn't he think of a kid sooner? That couple had a baby. He zooms in to Coco's hand on the boy's shoulder, hustling him along. The kid's not that excited about his midnight visit.

Human trafficking is what he decides, because that's the way his mind works in this business. That will certainly improve his report.

Chapter 34

THE DETRITUS of Reagan's mother's collection—what falls off the taxidermy and what goes bad, a lot of shoddy glass eyes, broken beak tips, and not a few feathers—is what she calls the remains. She is cataloging them, identifying each shred of torn skin and every handful of feathers with a name and a number, and entombing them in acid-free boxes. Access to these remains has always been sought by someone. Her mother's correspondence contains numerous letters from nightclub acts and movie stars willing to pay large sums for shoes featuring bird bits, feathered masks, and of course cloaks woven out of "leftovers." Today women weave pheasant feathers into their hair and strap full faux wings to the back of their evening wear, some not so faux. Fashion is once again recognizing the beauty of birds, after decades of hiatus.

Her own grandmother was photographed marching with the suffragists in front of the White House wearing a wildly feathered hat that sparked a nearly insatiable desire for feathers in thousands of women, and she made a fortune from it. She and her husband, the railroad magnate, consigned hunters in Florida to collect snowy egret feathers by any means possible, whole flocks of them, and a feud started up between hunters that resulted in the death of one when he was "mistaken" for a bird on the first day of shooting. Nonetheless, feathers were collected, and not just a few or the fallen. Two thousand dead pelicans were needed for a single robe. The military, too, went gaga and wore feathers for every occasion, especially the Turkish sultans with their outrageous turbans, the French with aigrette affixed to their helmets, and the British with their shako and hackle.

The club members want to exhibit these remains with everything else at the annual meeting. Not only would they show her mother's resplendent collection in memoriam but they'd highlight that nothing of the animals was ever wasted, that taxidermy was both elegant and efficient. While she granted that such an exhibit would be quite spectacular, she had her own ideas. The board was pressing against them, insisting she prepare the remains and the taxidermy, period. There was even talk of replacing her, the executive director told her sotto voce, because she, as the heir, for reasons of compliance with the tax code, should have more perceived distance from the decisions of the board.

She would mount the collection with the remains, yes, but instead of looking backward at dead animal displays, she would forge into the future. She was hoping to enlarge the photo she found on the internet and use it as a backdrop, but she can't find it anymore online and the print doesn't look as good blown up. A better image would have generated excitement and suspense and speculation, but not as pixelated random dots. You can't even imagine the flying woman in it without squinting. Tim said it looked more like a Rorschach test.

Very sophisticated of him.

She fires off an ultimatum.

Chapter 35

WHEN ROXY opens the door the next morning, Tim's nervous. He just sticks the little bouquet of carnations and roses out in front of him. Can I come in?

Few men know how effective clichés are, she says. She hesitates, tying a klutzy-looking bathrobe around her glittery pajamas. I stayed up all night working and am just now getting myself together.

I was worried when you didn't show up at the office.

Really? She smiles, accepting the flowers, her breasts pushing against the terry-cloth fold. So I took an unpaid sick day. I just saw you last night.

You need in-person sympathy. His hands empty now, he fumbles, tucks them behind his back. Sex pulses in his brain, and elsewhere.

They look at each other.

I'm not contagious, that's a plus, she says.

Out pops Chris from behind the kitchen door. Aha! Lovebirds, he says when he sees the flowers in her hands.

Roxy looks at Tim's feet.

I saw that you signed for him, says Tim, stiffening into his office self.

Go on, Chris. She hustles him toward the door. The bus stops the third block after the intersection. Coco will meet you at the shrink's office. Remember our agreement?

I forget nothing, he says in a robot voice. He gives Tim a meaningful glance.

Go on, you little punk, says Tim, but not without forcing a smile. You do know how to keep a secret, right?

You'll see, and Chris slams shut the door.

He's trouble, says Tim. I've seen him skateboarding outside my office. Heard him. He wouldn't move along.

He has plenty to deal with, says Roxy.

You know, you could be up for disciplinary action for having him here, he says, then clears his throat as if the sound alone could obliterate what he's just said.

Right, she says, laying the bouquet on the counter.

Anyway, don't worry about it. He touches her shoulder.

Okay, she says, looking him over. I'll put these in water. You want some coffee?

No, thanks, he says. I've already drunk the pot at work. He leans back on his heels while she pulls the blooms into an arrangement. He can't avoid looking into the overflowing bedroom. Small space, he says.

The apartment is too expensive to afford by myself. Coco sleeps on the couch.

Right, he says.

While she puts her coffee together, he takes a seat on the couch and throws his arm over the back, very casually. Then he remembers Coco sleeps there and stands up.

Bagel? It's got seeds, she says from the kitchen, and he refuses that too.

The toaster oven clicks on.

I'll just be another second. She backs into the bedroom and tries to close the door completely but two silver hangers on the floor won't let her. There's a pervert in the neighborhood, she calls out. Somebody sitting in a van.

Maybe it doesn't start. He peers through a window.

It's been there for weeks.

He checks out the rest of the place: knickknacks with wings, a marble ashtray that looks like a nest. They're slow to tow around here, he says.

She's changed into a skirt and jacket. In three minutes, she's holding the bagel in one hand, coffee in the other.

The flowers were a little over the top, I'll admit, he says, but I hoped they'd make an impression. Hands in pockets, he returns to the couch.

She nods over her mug, standing over him. He's cowed by her unblinking eyes. She drinks the whole mug down straight. Still watching him, she brushes a few magazines off the end of the couch and takes the seat beside him. Coco won't be home for hours, she says. She takes a bite of bagel.

He fusses with what's in his pocket. That probably seems nervous.

How about we go to lunch, he says. You know a place around here?

I'm eating now, she says, taking another bite.

I want to talk to you, he says, about Coco.

Really?

He leans over her and whispers: It's like this, but instead of going on, he kisses her so well she responds, he puts his arms around her, then he moves his hands over her breasts—and she groans with her eyes shut.

Tidbitting is what some birds do, she whispers, opening her dark eyes. Very romantic. Pick up food or pretend to, and offer it.

He pinches his fingers together and tucks an imaginary treat into her mouth, then kisses her again, touches her all over while keeping his wrist never far from her face. She nuzzles the corner of his neck, then licks his palm.

It tickles.

He whispers and she whispers, and they kiss long and hard. She's not going to bite him. At least he hopes not. He's inflamed by the possibility of sex with her, he's terrified by it.

She turns away, in invitation, her back to him—her skirt twisted to her waist, and he wriggles inside, grasps her breasts for traction. Attraction, he thinks, if he thinks. He is avian himself then, reptilian even, grasping and groping and she's happy about it, he's sure, she's loud, so loud, screeching—and he's finished. A few seconds later her wings judder. At least that's what he thinks is nestled between her shoulders still hidden under that jacket, and she makes a sound that's quick and quiet—a mew. A few feathers float around them. He moves his arm out from under her, rubs it where it's gone to sleep, then slides his hand around and over her belly and thinks he feels something.

She shoves him almost off the couch.

Whew, he says, tucking and zipping, I'm exhausted.

Men, she says, sitting up. A man. She spits that out like a real man-hater.

Yes, he says. I am a man.

A man's penis is so much shorter.

Is that an insult? he laughs just a tiny bit.

Hey, answer me, he says.

Her silence causes fear to flood him as quickly as the sensuous had, a charge, this one a wave too big to ride. She holds him there with her eyes, and her silence.

He pulls her face close again for another kiss.

She tries to push him away but he's got the hypodermic shoved in already, she screams and writhes and stares at him while he pushes the plunger, her talons flexing in the air—what happened to her hands?—just as she goes limp in his arms.

He touches her blonde hair, the long neck, her dark lashes, the bouquet of feathers he discovers bursting from the back of her jacket, he wants to nestle his face between those feathery breasts he uncovers, he actually lies down next to her, breathing her in—and again remembers the snake and the condor.

He drags the furniture and all the other stuff off the rug and rolls her into it. That's not exactly what you're supposed to do with your lover after sex, but there you are. He's sweating by the time he gets her all organized. What if she can't breathe? He loosens the carpet but not too much or she'll fly. Really? He flings open the cupboard doors. Stacked cups, towels, a bag of clip-closed birdseed. He checks the brand then empties it into the trash, fits the bag over her shoes and bungee-cords it tight around her ankles.

He wipes down the fingerprints.

He should take the stairs but it's too many flights down. He hauls the carpet to the elevator. He hasn't lugged a woman around since when—since that whole threshold thing with his first wife. The second one he threw over his shoulder and they both fell to the ground laughing. She got hysterical. He should have known it wasn't going to work out.

This one weighs so little.

Chapter 36

IF YOU find a baby bird, you have to leave it alone, I tell Chris. If you touch it, the mother won't claim the chick anymore. That's not true with a cat or a raccoon.

The boy is looking through a picture book about a lost bird. He's way too old for that kind of book but that's all they have in the shrink's waiting room, and he doesn't want to engage with me. The medication from last night is wearing off and he's getting restless. My mother's dead, he says.

He sounds as if he's running the idea past me, testing it. That's too bad, I say.

He peels a scab away from a dirt-rimmed wound inflicted by a pen or pencil that's festering on the back of his hand. Is my dad going to die too?

You sound hopeful.

The kid flinches. Are you a therapist? Maybe you can give me pills that I can hide in my cheek and sell later.

Smart ass.

The kid snaps the book shut. Drugs change me into

someone else. Is that someone the one I'm supposed to be or am I the right one already? Which?

What did your dad say?

He doesn't know anything. I thought you would. You're different.

Thanks, I say. I don't ask if he means that I'm sensitive to his situation, or if he suspects my difference is more fundamental.

The nurse waves his chart. Chris opens the book again, pretends to be completely absorbed. The doctor's only going to talk to you, says the nurse. No needles.

He's offended by being treated like a baby, but he's acting like one. I have to tow him into the doctor's office. The shrink at the door smiles and asks Chris if he feels comfortable talking with him alone. Chris has no problem with that.

When he's through, I offer him a coat that I brought from a bin we keep at the office for emergencies. Spring's turned chilly again. He's looking a little dazed, even more close-mouthed than before. Lethe, he says on the way out. Lethe, Lethe. The shrink thought I was saying *meth-y*.

You mispronounced it. It's *Lee-thee*.

Ha, he says.

That's the kind of thing you might learn at school.

No way, he says. Besides, you just told me.

Chris is in no hurry to visit his dad. A guilty conscience? I leave him with a nurse at check-in. He's not going to run because he wants to know how his dad is doing, but he doesn't want to face him. Does he also hesitate because he suspects his father has told on him? But on admittance, his dad said he fell off the couch, nothing about anybody hitting him over the head.

I haven't forgotten how Chris lifted the lamp over me.

There's nothing new on his father's chart. He's said nothing about the boy. He must be afraid they'll be separated. I don't inquire about his injuries. I assure him we're taking good care of his son. Whatever Chris did must be on his mind because he scratches at a tuft of gray hair sticking out from the gauze around his head and says it was nobody's fault. Things happen.

He got crazy after he hit you and then went out and found trouble with some other kids, right? He was picked up by the police, you know.

I heard from Stewie you took him in, he mutters. He grips both sides of his bandaged head as if he's suffering from a bad headache.

Which is quite possible.

That's way beyond social services, that's kind, he says.

I didn't want you worrying about him, I say.

He turns toward the dividing curtain in the room. It's my fault, he says, his voice breaking. I just can't control him. There must be something wrong with me.

Fault isn't useful, I say. We're getting more help for him, and for you too. Where is his mother?

He shifts his gaze to his covers and buries his hands

under them as if they were suddenly cold. The social worker a year ago said if we didn't get along and one of us didn't move out, then she'd have to take the boy away. We were thankful she put it to us like that because some of the social workers just ask which one is moving out and when neither party budges, the next thing you know, they're at the door with the police to take the kid away.

I take a big breath. Stupid.

He agrees. Then I was alone with the problem. Oh, I couldn't manage both of them anyway. He flexes his gnarled hands. She was trouble too, like the boy.

It runs in families. Get some rest, I say.

He's not really nuts, says his father. He's too young.

The young can be sick too.

Yeah, I guess. Can I borrow your phone? he asks. Mine's out of juice and I can't lose this job.

I listen to his side of the conversation. He does props and is looking for rodeo gear—silver belt buckles and spurs—for a big musical number.

Chapter 37

THEY WANT him to come in.

Robinson's sitting in his living room, no kids, the wife and them all settled back in their shelter, the camera in the van running solo for an hour, dog cam on him. He watches himself look around the room at the discarded toys his wife didn't manage to collect, the dog asleep on his dirty shirt on the floor.

They want him to come in? The only time the office asks you to come is to hire or fire.

Probably they just laughed when they looked at the footage. You're pulling the old rabbit with antelope horns trick, is what they must think, photoshopping whatever was in his fevered little brain just to get out of the van and collect unemployment. Everybody knows there's doctored media. He can doctor media. That's what he should have done in the first place.

Where are his shoes? They ought to be putting the A team on this, Special Operations French Navy Seals, that's as much as he knows. Although, what? He played that foot-age of her over and over, and did he believe it?

He could try again.

He's never had a job disappear on him, never.

He won't go in right away. What would be the point? She's still out and about.

He reviews the contents of the fridge. He was intending to pack peanut butter and jelly and a couple of nice jerky sticks, maybe a coke, for surveillance time but it's empty, cleaned out by the kids.

Probably the office only wants to terminate his contract and put on somebody else.

He refills the dog feeder.

Forget any more footage. All he needs is a really good solid clue or a better motive to convince them to keep him on. Why is the fugitive spending so much time at the hospital? Hard to know what she does in the interior of buildings without getting out of the van and possibly losing her. You can hypothesize a movie if they go into a theater, groceries at the grocers, but a big place like a hospital? She could be scouting locations on the roof for another homicide, she could be getting fitted for another head. Or feathers.

He nibbles on the kibble. It's not bad, but gritty. Must clean the dog's teeth. His wife's eggs were like that, bits of shell.

Does he miss her? A little.

Some people—like him—really just like to watch, they don't want to go in, hand to hand. He'll tell the office he has a hunch about the suspect to do with trafficking that will confirm everything they've seen. They'll look into it but keep him on to monitor the situation. Maybe even increase his pay since the recent defenestrations happened so close, and trafficking is getting a lot of play.

His wife calls. You should sell her picture on the dark web.

I should never have told you about her.

The money would help the kids—people pay a lot for photos like that. I could get out of this place with some cash. We could go home together.

Home is where the heart is, he says after a while.

I'm not asking to move back in with you, she says. You can work in your filthy van all alone for as long as you like. You should be happy I never told my boyfriend your name, and that he never thought to look for us at your place. Battered women? He thinks that's something you fry.

He hangs up.

He'll bring in that bird on his own if he has to, no problem.

Chapter 38

HERE YOU go, says Tim, hoisting her onto the examination table.

Awfully small wings. Reagan taps her nails against a full wine glass.

She had big enough wings when I gave her the shot. It's not my fault she had a reaction. Why not wait until the drug wears off to judge? Or at least until she comes to.

Reagan steps closer and peers over her glass. Fascinating.

He starts unbuttoning her skirt, pulling at her blouse. What was in that shot? She's been unconscious for at least two hours. He very gently slides the blouse off one arm and then the other. It took me that long to get her in the van, drive the speed limit through all those little towns, and figure out the code on your gate.

You should've figured out the code easily. Isn't that what private investigators do?

In the movies.

He wrestles off the last of her clothing. Nice, he says under his breath. The nipples, thrust between tiny white curling feathers, the soft *v* of her nethers. Completely stripped, she's shockingly beautiful, covered in iridescent pink and green feathers. Just a glance at the down of her décolleté and he's excited all over again. He couldn't really look before, he was so rushed—or afraid. He drops her panties to the floor.

A real examination room.

I wonder if she enjoys Halloween. Reagan stands over her, lights a cigarette, waves the smoke around as if it should be shared.

Without taking his eyes off all the glorious plumage, he says: I'll take the rest of my fee now.

She exhales. Did you give her water?

She's been unconscious, remember? Do you have a blanket? She looks cold.

She has feathers. You just have to be sure she gets plenty of liquids. Reagan splashes a bit of wine from the glass she's holding onto the captive's face. That's good rosé, she says.

A tongue appears, catches a few drops.

See? says Reagan. Sit her up.

I don't have time for a lot of fooling around, he says as evenly as possible. I have to get back to work by four. He wrestles her upright and dabs the wine dribble off her face with a paper towel from a dispenser. The money?

Reagan riffles through her bird-covered tote, around the

open bottle of wine, along with probably the pistol, and what else? She hands him a fat envelope. Count it.

While Reagan examines the bird on her own, Tim lays the hundreds in piles on the counter behind them. Every bill fills him with remorse. How he longs to run his hands over the bird again, to hold her close, to confess—the very word frightens him—the love he has for her, he really does have it. Such an emotion has never washed over him before, he's drowning in it—and now that's all ruined. The cash isn't the same as having her. He's surprised by how high the piles get, and how little he cares.

You're satisfied? she says.

He says nothing, tucks the bulge of bills into his jacket.

She should come around pretty soon, she says. Give her some more to drink. It might improve her wings. Then take her into the aviary. I have one more job for you on this project.

He's not sure he wants another job from her but, what the hell, he'll have more time with Roxy.

This time he supports her head, puts the glass to her mouth. She hisses without opening her eyes.

Oh, a troublemaker. Reagan leans very close. Kissy, kissy, she says, and smacks her lips. Pretty bird.

The harpy's head darts forward, knocking the wine away, and bites a chunk out of Reagan's cheek.

He almost laughs.

After Reagan stops screaming, a paper towel clutched

to her face, she digs out plastic cuffs from deep in her tote. Both hands and feet, she says and pulls a fresh paper towel off the roll to replace the blood-soaked one. This is what I get for helping humanity.

He's clumsy—every touch over her downy self inflames him.

Is this little chore too hard for you? Reagan asks, practically tapping her foot. Do I have to do it? She lifts the tote from the floor and holds it to her chest. She wants him to think about another envelope of money, yes, but also that little pistol.

Tim lowers Roxy onto the bark-covered floor next to some kind of weird berry bush and unwraps her from the blanket he found in the van. He positions a syringe full of sedative a few feet away, just in case, and clips off the plastic around her hands and legs.

She rolls onto her elbows, she squats for a moment, orienting herself. A trail of feathers wisps to the ground.

He holds his wrist to her face. Sweetheart, he says, and he catches an elbow to steady her rise. We can do it again.

No need. This morning was enough.

Enough for what? he says.

She's standing, brushing her feathers. I think there's a few things your keeper—she pauses—hasn't told you.

Very funny, my keeper.

Well, she says. Who's calling the shots?

I'm calling this one. He holds his wrist to her face again. Breathe in.

She beats away his arm. How is whatever chemical you're wearing different from a roofie?

He takes her by the shoulders, he looks right into those dark dark eyes of hers. What we did was not rape. He shakes her. You love me, he says. I know this, he continues, with a strength that surprises him. And I love you.

You're right, she says, you are actually right. But you just drugged and kidnapped me. She jerks her head away to stop him from kissing her. For money.

Those eyes.

You want me to propose, get all mushy and tell you I've got a little nest all picked out for you? One hook-up and that's what you want?

His voice is soft, so soft.

She leans toward him and just when he puts his arms out to hold her, she plucks a feather from the side of his neck. He flinches. You know what size my egg's going to be?

No, he says. Egg?

It's going to be too big, she says in a voice he hasn't heard before. Then she lunges, what's left of the crushed wings flare, she comes at him, her teeth bare. Large teeth. She hisses.

He's too afraid to do anything but put up his wrist again. She holds her breath.

Love, she spits out, and with two or three strong wing

strokes, despite all the feathers she's lost, she pumps her wings big, she's high in the air in a second, her hair streaming behind her, claws full out. Then she dives to the emergency exit, shoves it open with her shoulder, the alarm ringing instantly.

Who would've thought a bird would use the exit?

I'll get Coco, he yells before it closes.

The elevator whirrs down from the third floor, then Reagan's standing in front of him. She crosses her arms and taps her forefinger to her chin. I have microphones.

Now you know. He turns away from her to stare out the window.

She won't get far, says Reagan. She's weak, the egg will sap whatever strength she has. An egg, she says, with rapture. But this Coco you threatened her with, who's that?

Get away, he says.

Chapter 39

CHRIS'S FATHER has to stay in the hospital at least another night. I might as well be taken for a dollar as a dime, with regard to the rules, so I bring Chris to my place again. He's still a bit unstable, I can see it in his eyes when I pick him up from school, they wander and settle, but he's been prescribed a better set of pills, though it will take time for them to take effect. Yes, there will be a trust issue to work out between father and son, but after talking straight to the doctors, his dad understands better where the violence comes from and what to do about it.

I unlock our door. Oh my god.

Chris follows me in. No way, he says.

All the furniture's shoved around, feathers are fear-molted everywhere, the whole place is torn up. Must've been angry at a pillow, says Chris.

I check the window. The van hasn't moved, though now the windshield features an unconvincing *Emergency* sign.

Chris shoves the couch into its corner. He's worn out

from the mostly sleepless night and skateboarding the afternoon away, but he's not going to let me ignore the situation. Your sister gets really angry?

Like you? is what I should say regarding the attack on his father, but I don't. At least I have a scrap of patience left for him. She's not the angry type, I tell him. Just not so good with housekeeping.

Ha, he says. He pushes again at the couch. I was here this morning, you know.

I'm shaking. I go right over to the fridge and stick my head inside and find cookie dough. I could've pulled out a vat of sour cream, I'm that upset. Hungry?

I could eat all that before it even gets in the oven, he says, right behind me.

I look at the cylinder of dough. I blink. Not a good idea.

He grabs the dough and taps me on the head with it. I flinch, having a flashback of him trying to kayo me with the lamp.

I'm like confused when I take these pills, he says, looking around for something he can use to cut open the cylinder. Or when I don't.

It's hard to get the pills right, I say, as automatically as I can. I hand him a dinner knife. Your body is always changing. It gets better sometimes when you get older. People do live reasonable lives being bipolar.

Yeah, he says. Sure. You don't trust me with something sharper?

Trust doesn't come out of nowhere.

You'll see, he says. He hacks into the cookie dough with much enthusiasm. So, where's your sister? He eats a raw gob off the tip.

I don't know, I say slowly, eyeing the bouquet, tossing a half-eaten bagel into the trash, looking around for something decent for Chris to eat. I slam shut the cupboard stuffed with all the seed. Okay, let's try you out, Mr. Detective. What do you see here?

Crime scene, he says. A lot of pushed-over stuff. And, he says, with triumph, no rug. You had one.

Very good.

Maybe she's been kidnapped.

I can't go to the police.

He sits up. Write a note for me for school. Dad won't mind. I'll do a complete investigation.

Chris has probably watched a lot more media than I have and will have more hunches about how kidnappers operate, plus all kinds of suppositions about where she's gone and how to rescue her. But the media is best at distortion, not solution. At the beginning of one-reelers, I got so interested in a crazy car chase, I flew at the screen and hit my head and fell into the front row. Thank god, the audience was so wrapped up in the picture themselves, they didn't really notice.

He stops gouging at the dough to consider the situation. Is she, like, a dealer?

Nope, guess again, I say, putting a frozen enchilada in the microwave, thinking how that explanation would simplify everything, that maybe that's the closest analogy—flying as a drug. Hard to share, though.

No police, huh? You could just rush in and get her back, commando style, he says. That's how you're supposed to do it anyway.

I call the super.

He says the guy he saw with the rug was tall, dark, and handsome like all the guys girls like you date. You didn't want it cleaned? You'll have to report it stolen.

It was old anyway, I say. I don't say how old.

It's breaking and entering. You don't want that to happen again. One of you girls home alone—

You're right, I say. Now that I think about it, of course we sent the rug out. I just forgot.

He sighs with exasperation. Call me any time, he says. Except after 5 p.m. Like now. He hangs up.

I poke the still-cold enchilada with a fork and put it back in the microwave, I hold my hand out for what's left of the dough.

Chris pinches off another gob before giving it up. You need me to go in after her. Nobody would suspect me. He flops down on the couch, licking more dough off his fingers.

Maybe, I say. I retrieve a cookie sheet from the cupboard, I check a text on my phone. They're letting your dad out tomorrow morning. He's pretty old to get beaten up. Are you sure you don't want to be an orphan?

He's not on the couch anymore; he's found the ball again

in a corner, and he's bouncing it. Heroes are always orphans. Batman, Superman.

Superman's parents were from another planet.

That's the way it always is, he says, tossing the ball high into the air. On another planet. And it's our job to make sure they stay there.

You didn't make that up. I offer the warmed-up enchilada, which he ignores.

No, he says, there's this game on my phone—

I catch the ball as it comes down in front of me. If you're not going to eat, go start your homework.

He doesn't go near his backpack, he begins circling the room, starting to get really wound up. I can tell you one thing—I'll bet she got rolled into the carpet.

I don't say that only happens in cartoons, I do say, you are definitely on the case. Very cool. But this is how we're going to make this work for both of us: you're going to eat some dinner and, okay, some cookies, do your homework, go to school tomorrow, then your dad's coming home, and you're going home with him, not me. You'll text me with your progress on the case and we'll swap notes. And you're not going to tell anyone about it.

He wedges the ball into his mouth and flails his hands as if he can't say a word to me or anybody else, then spits it out. I saw that guy from your office here yesterday morning.

Really? I say.

Lovebirds, he says. Fucking lovebirds.

Chapter 40

TIM SCANS every fir-and-leaf-covered tree in the neighborhood with a pair of binoculars he found in a drawer in the reception area. Roxy's been gone all night. Was she going to hang around just because he was a great lover? He's not so keen on bringing in Coco, that's for sure, but it was the only thing he could think of to say at the time that he thought might stop Roxy from flying off. Now he's beating the bushes all the way to the main road, using the stock of the tranq gun Reagan gave him. Three were hanging on the wall outside the aviary. The rifle-looking one he took must be for ostriches, the pistol more like for eagles? The other for hummingbirds?

When you grow up you can have a real gun, Reagan said when she found him inspecting them the day before. You wimp, she'd said, after he told her he refused to carry a firearm. You could always shoot yourself with one of these tranq numbers to see if they're lethal.

Good suggestion.

Nonetheless, she showed him how to arm it with darts filled with some sedative or nerve toxin. He took the stun pistol too, because why not? They're single shot. Boy, they sure look like real guns to him.

He wants to catch Roxy for himself, not for Reagan, he wants to apologize to her, to somehow make up for the situation, to take her home to his place. But he doesn't want to shoot her out of some tree, where she might hurt herself, falling. He's found some of the birdseed he'd fed to the peacock at the zoo deep in his pocket and has brought along a blanket.

What exactly is going to happen to her? he'd asked Reagan on his way out.

She flashed one of her less attractive smiles. If you bring her in, I promise to give her the best of care.

That did not console him.

Birds sing everywhere he turns. Sneaking up on Roxy is not an option. It's like having a bunch of alarms going off with his every step. He moves away from the trees into the middle of the road and stares back at the noisy birds, singing and shrieking in the branches as if signaling her, he thinks, as if they know where she's hiding.

He waves his guns at them, and they fly.

Well, Roxy's not going to wander into town naked, with her wings hanging out. She has to be in here somewhere.

Naked, he keeps that vision of her foremost.

Chapter 41

ROBINSON STARES at his corkboard with its tangle of red thread and old photos. He discards the outliers, including the Frenchman's nephew, in another attempt—his fourth? his twentieth?—to see what they have in common. If you have your motive, you have your perp. Trafficking, really? This is Detective 101 and surely Interpol, or whoever, has already been down that alley—and even if he discovers something, they will not be grateful, they will not jump into their high-speed chase cars or fly over to congratulate him. Administration here was certainly dour when he finally showed up. An officer of few words and little patience heard his story. Robinson told him surveillance is all about imagination and persistence, just give him a little more time, he has a hunch but he has to keep it to himself, for now. Never mind the footage. Ha, ha, he said.

What else could he do?

The officer scoffed, the officer threatened, and in the end, as he predicted, the officer fired him.

He called his wife to offer his key again because he's decided to stay in the van until he cracks the case, period. But when she heard the office wasn't paying, she said she'd better stay put, she didn't want to be involved in an eviction.

He discovers some of the victims' families offer rewards online, if that's what *récompense* means in French, and google says so. More motive for him, if not justice, which he should be caring a lot about but sees not a lot of it happening. It's more like he needs to clear his good name on this one.

The van is ready and willing. He removes the emergency sign he put up while pondering his firing. Not that he's angry. He's been trained in anger management. Doing surveillance has a lot in common with having an assignment on one of those military submarines. You have to keep bottled whatever you feel. He's glad now that he doesn't have a partner in the van—he'd have to split the reward and they might quarrel—although he could use another set of eyes. The work is close and tedious, like most things that stay in the dark.

Six of the victims were found with coupons for a certain grand opening, but the whole region was inundated with coupons that day. Looked at another way, there were ten more men than women in this group and the men probably weren't coupon clippers, but he still does a lot of noodling around the grand opening, the *grande ouverture* of what appears to be discount children's bikes.

A red herring if he ever saw one.

He returns to calculating the demographics, the lists of rationales. What about money? Nobody got robbed, and none of the victims appear to have much in the bank except the nephew running the sex ring and he's out. Too obviously an inside job. He looks more closely at the rest of them. Children. That would go with trafficking and that's one common denominator that the cops would overlook. And Coco's in social services, in contact with plenty of them.

Somebody—somebody with very tiny fingers—has fooled with the screen of his endoscopic camera when that someone sat on his lap. He'd spent a lot of one night clinging to the side of Coco's apartment building, dressed in ninja black, drilling a tiny hole in the window casement for the camera so he could see inside. And what did he see after he so carefully rappelled down and heaved himself back into the van? The back of a couch. He intends to try again and reposition the camera but hasn't found the energy. Now the couch has been moved to one side. How exciting! There's Coco, there's the boy, and he's bouncing a ball against the wall just above the lens. A signal for help?

On the second bounce, the ball hits the lens hard. Cracks it.

He crosses his arms, considers the photo again.

Maybe he should practice catching some of the bigger birds and work his way up?

Chapter 42

CHRIS FALLS right to sleep after the cookie course. His new drugs are very effective in that area, but still I whisper-call the local hospital and the morgue, I open the back window and leave seed on the sill, I yell *Roxy!* into the night, hoping she will come winging through it. She has before.

Then I jump out one of the windows—might as well, this late—and zoom high, very high, tucking my legs under, imitating whatever big bird has been around recently, diving and whistling *Wait-a-Minute, Wait-a-Minute*, our emergency signal.

No dice. I'm glad it's not close to hunting season.

No sign of Tim at his place. I rip open a window screen to make sure: a tuxedo jacket zipped into a suit bag like a trophy, cummerbund dropped on the couch but half-covered with old circulars and receipts as if he wasn't planning on wearing it again for another decade, and a lot of bird books.

I get the books, but formal wear?

It's not exactly sleep that I enjoy back at our apartment, and it's still dark when I wake up. I'm on edge. I defrost a muffin covered with the pecans Roxy loves. Chris carefully picks off every one, and I drink a cup of tea, too tired and wired to object or eat anything myself. I deliver him early to school. He's very unhappy about that but he's never happy at school. On the way to work, I extract one of those beautiful iridescent white feathers from my breast—it practically kills me—and drop it in the park, and then I ogle the swan swimming across the lake at the end, thinking XXL breakfast. I'm warbling under my breath to lure it closer when two birders come at me with a microphone rig. What's that call? Pileated woodpecker? says the one with the fanciest binoculars. Can it be?

Ivory-billed woodpecker, says the second one. They haven't been seen anywhere since 2004.

I give them my best withering glance. Just as they start walking backward, staring at the treetops with their binoculars, I imitate a Florida grasshopper sparrow, a nice little bird even more recently endangered. That stops them cold. I saunter past while they get frantic, emptying a backpack for what I assume is a special recording device since one of them dangles a thin length of cable.

Ten minutes later I stroll the park as a birder myself, notebook under my armpit, glasses and a squint, free to tweet at will, whenever. The other two still stand there, alert and unmoving, as if they were stuffed, surrounded by their devices, talking about turbines and how dangerous they are to birds.

I pretend to be a competing birder and ignore them.

I don't even want to think about things like turbines, but I have to. New threats to us turn up all the time. Plane engines clogging up with birds, that sort of thing. What if Roxy and I actually are the last? Truganini, the last indigenous Tasmanian—her mother killed by sailors, her uncle shot by a soldier, her sister abducted by sealers, and her fiancé brutally murdered by timber cutters, who then repeatedly sexually abused her—begged to have her remains buried and not dissected, but only two years after her death, her skeleton went on display. Or there's Ishi, last of the Yahi, kept on exhibit in a museum by the University of California. When asked his name, Ishi said: I have none, because I had no people to name me.

Me, me, me, me sings a species, until there's no one to listen. We'll hit the dissection table faster than water can boil.

I scrutinize every feather I come across, every pillow escapee. Where are you? I text.

Robinson's harassing some fat goose—for feathers?—at the far end of the park. I decide a bus is the safest way to get to the office.

Stewie catches me punching in. It's almost lunchtime, he says, hauling files down the hall toward Tim, who's picking through an armload at the end of it.

Chris took a long time getting out of the van. That kid can really talk.

We sure could use you to help with the upgrade, Tim interrupts, tossing a big bunch of files into recycling.

I take a deep breath. I could kill Tim but would that get me closer to Roxy? You're throwing away everything? I say. It's come to that?

No more paper at all. Every move documented online. Transparency, Tim says, as soon as we can reconfigure the interface.

Is that like trance-parenting? Parenting with your eyes closed? says Stewie.

I've seen that, I say. I give Tim my coldest stare.

Tim laughs, but too loud. He crouches down to collect some files in the bottom drawers. How's Roxy feeling? he says to the floor. She didn't come in today.

What should I say? Tim was last seen with Roxy, let's call the police? She's much better, thank you, I lie.

He knows that I know.

Stewie ducks out the door for more files.

I'm about to text my sister again when a very thick file escapes Tim's nervous hand and papers fall everywhere. "8-year-old dies of skull fracture" reads the heading of the one at my feet. I pick it up while Tim gathers the rest of the pages. Sixty complaints, according to the investigators. I'm appalled more than usual. This kid was forced to write his own suicide note, I tell Tim, pointing at the document.

How can they prove he was forced? Come on.

Down there—I point lower on the page—his teacher said he turned it in as homework. He didn't want to embarrass his mother with misspellings.

Tim skims the page while feeding more paper into the shredder. I noticed it also says they couldn't get a warrant against the mother because the boy kept taking back his story.

Are you saying the boy was dishonest?

Tim says no in a strained voice, he's saying maybe a kid has only one mom and what's he supposed to do?

Ha! The deposition says the mom shot a BB gun into his face. He had clumps of hair pulled out. What kind of mom did you have?

That is an unprofessional question. Tim is holding the files in front of him as if they will ward off more.

Is all this digital conversion just a coincidence? I ask. Does this case and some special-problem others have something to do with all this shredding? I hold up the boy's file.

A different office handles the really tough cases, he says, emptying what's left of the documents into a garbage bag.

Ahem, Stewie interrupts, going for another batch of files. He hates all conflict in the office. There's enough of it on his workload.

At least Tim's not gloating. I want to throw my phone at him anyway, but if I throw it, my sister can't text me. I look at the phone face instead of his.

Nothing. I text her again.

I return to my cubicle and move the files on my desk

from one side to the other, the few that are left, I open and close their covers as if they need air. I want to read them all before they're scanned so I'll know something about what's being eliminated.

I don't read a thing.

An hour later, Tim bustles into my cubicle while I'm peeling the pesticides off an apple.

You look sick, I say. Kind of hunchbacky, and pale. Maybe even pimply. You're never going to get Roxy that way. If you haven't already. I try a fake smile.

Come into my office, says Tim.

So seductive, I say. You trust me to be alone with you?

Tim goes into recoil mode, but he's got a quick recovery: You cannot say things like that here or I'll file for harassment.

It usually doesn't work that way.

He glares at me until I follow him. Once inside his office, he offers me his spare chair.

No, thanks, I'll stand. Whatever you have to say won't take long. What is it?

He searches through the papers on his desk. He says, without looking up: The police called. The minute the father got out of the hospital, Chris beat him up all over again. You need to get over there.

That cannot be true. They were getting along fine. Besides, why didn't you just text me?

He comes around his desk with a paper in his hand.

You're so crazy about paper, I knew you wouldn't believe me without a report. Here it is.

The report, about five minutes old, shows Chris off his meds, fighting with his dad straight out of the hospital, signed by Tim.

Why don't you send Stewie?

Retrieving the document, Tim pauses as if he were trying to remember just who Stewie is. Distracted? He grips another fat file on his desk and tosses it into his wastebasket. Stewie's gone to get another shredder. You'll have to drive a van over by yourself.

I certainly won't take a van, I don't say as I walk out.

But first I have to get the keys to make it look as if I am taking a van. I'm already inside the storeroom where they are kept, staring at all the little labeled hooks, thinking, Oh, but if I fly then the van will still be in the lot and everyone will wonder, when a bag goes over my head and a needle into my neck.

Chapter 43

MESSIAEN BIRDSONG of trumpets and rumbling tim-
pani, *Wings of Desire,* the wingless German guys in ugly
overcoats, *putti* conniving against all the adults in a painting or else pulling them apart, bickering bickering bickering, a weeping angel statue lifting a hand off the crypt, time
stretched slo-mo slooooooow-mo, *gone batty*—

Chapter 44

BY EAR is the phrase I've heard used if you don't have a plan. I prefer *winging it*.

Only by being captured will I find my sister. If it's Tim, or if it's that guy from the white van, Robinson, whatever—I've muddled out this at least, the drug in me making it hard to reason much further. *Gone batty*. Papers—reports, drafts, excel spreadsheets, most of it shredded—fill the canvas mail cart I've been dumped into that's jammed into the back of a van. One of the vans I wasn't going to take. Papers cover my head—I've been disguised by my work.

Okay.

Tim's voice comes in and out from the front seat. He must be driving, and who's that—Chris?

How do you know she's a bird for sure? His voice is high. Scared.

I'm her supervisor, says Tim.

I pull at my restraints. Tight. The paper shifts when he takes a curve, and my head's out.

Oh, says Chris. So you always knew. I heard Roxy talk about stuff to Coco once, but I didn't think everybody knew.

What did they say?

Nothing really, says Chris. Tweet, tweet.

I smile.

But why tie up Coco? says Chris. She's cool.

Birds get the flu, says Tim, and it's dangerous. She needs to be treated for her own good, and maybe ours. She might not want to.

Why not? asks Chris. After Tim says nothing, and we careen around another corner, Chris says: Did you know they're sisters?

Really? says Tim. That makes things a lot easier.

Why?

Same vaccine.

Oh, says Chris.

We ride on. Almost nighttime. Few lights reflected on the van's ceiling. A long way from the city. My feet are numb. I wiggle my toes.

You told Dad I was going to the shrink's, says Chris.

Hey, you got out of school. You don't like school much, do you?

No, says Chris, I don't. I was going to buy a gun and shoot the school up, kill all the teachers, but Dad says everybody's a school shooter these days, why bother.

That gets Tim's attention. You're not into that, are you?

The van takes another curve too fast. There's the sound

of a skateboard rolling around under the seats. The kid doesn't answer. Smart kid.

I'm thinking not of myself as kidnapped, but Chris. How much money was Tim paid to do this? How desperate is he? There'll be plenty of time to find out, time enough for trouble to test him, time to meet whoever's in charge. I have met them before: sultans, hucksters with money in performance, once a Roman emperor who really preferred midgets. Often a private contractor. A man with a Tommy gun who told me to take off my costume.

I hear Chris unbuckling, turning in his seat to check on me. I wriggle a finger through the papers so he knows I'm okay. She's sleeping, he says, his voice louder.

But she looks really sick, he says, turning back. Take it easy on the curves. Then he starts talking nonstop in an even higher voice about whatever, until the drug puts me back to sleep.

I don't want to go in, Chris protests, and a lot of other things.

Quiet, says Tim. Get the door.

The back of the van opens up, a ramp gets banged down, then I'm wheeled out, and the door of the van's slammed shut and locked. Chris skitters around the side of the car. My board! he shouts. It's under the seat.

After we get her in, he says, we'll come back for it.

There's an edge to his voice that Chris must hear, or is he threatening him with something? I can't open my eyes to find out. Chris says nothing else and we take off over a gravel-strewn entrance—I can hear the crunch—and I peek. There's a lit-up three-story castle-like building of exquisite toned-down taste with an even taller aviary attached to it, and a supporting office block. That's what I think the building connected to the aviary's glass bubble must be, the one we're headed into.

Tim punches numbers into a keypad. Chris holds the door open and then I'm in, *thump, thump.* Lights turn on automatically down the corridor and flick off as we move forward, with Chris nonstop talking again. Where are we going? Where are the doctors? Where are the nurses? You said at least there would be doctors. You're her supervisor.

I almost smile, hearing rising annoyance in Tim's answering grunts. The room we end up in has a sink, a stainless steel table, and linoleum. I flex my feet in my shoes where the talons are folded but I don't otherwise move.

Shouldn't we let her loose? says Chris, in the midst of another jumble of sentences.

This bird is dangerously sick, says Tim. I have to examine her. He dumps me out of the cart onto the table, unzips my jacket, drags off my blouse, skirt, then carefully loosens the restraints around my limp ankles to pull off my shoes and socks, and only then does he cinch the restraints back on. Hurts.

Wow, says Chris. Look at her feet!

Tim angles me back into the cart. Yeah, those could really rip you apart.

I'm a little embarrassed, claws out, sitting here in just feathers. But I do have feathers.

The two of them gawk at me in my pretend sleep until Chris starts talking again, feverishly, about feet and talons and soft down in pillows. Ultralite, he says, touching my shoulder. Ultra-ultra.

You just stay here and watch that she doesn't get worse, Tim tells him. I'll be back with a specialist.

I hear a bolt thrown, locking us in.

Chapter 45

I'VE GOT her sister, Tim says. This kid too.

You ass, Reagan spits out in a cramped furious voice. It's the first bird we need, she's already inseminated, although I was going to have it done artificially. She paces back and forth.

This time they're inside the aviary house, in a room with one of those old-fashioned domed skylights and French doors overlooking the aviary extension. It's really late, and her cheek is red at the edge of her bandage. It looks hot and infected.

The woman is covered with feathers too, he says.

Feathers! she shrieks. I don't want feathers. She stops at a table with a framed photo of what must have been her as a child, holding an egg. Hoaxes have been arranged, she says, where determined and financially challenged taxidermists have pieced together chicken wings and glued on feathers to suggest new species. I have a whole case full of remains good for that kind of thing. There are anomalies possible too. Scientists in general are loath to admit anything truly unusual. She looks through him as if she's forgotten he's there. But you can't fake an egg. I need to have that first bird back here before she lays. I don't know how long that will take, and we don't know anything about your hypothetical second one.

Go look for yourself.

She touches her bandage. Even if this second one is a bird, she hasn't been around you as long as the other. Another insemination might not work. My presentation is in just a few days. She looks him up and down. You could have another try, I guess.

Seduce her?

That's not what birds do. You are so interspecies-ist.

Is that an insult?

She lowers her voice. If the subsequent breeding goes well, she says, I could cut you in. You could even have a vest made like the big operators and smuggle eggs to buyers like they do for those Malays with the gray parrots. Although the situation is not ideal on those long flights. Sometimes they break. Then what do you have? Eggshell everywhere, yolk. Good for nothing. Of course, this egg might be a bit too big for a vest. It could be very large.

Hold on, he says. You actually don't want the bird?

Just the egg. Her clenched fists say *want, want, want*. You can have her between broods.

He zips up his leather jacket. We'll see how that goes. I haven't had any luck finding her, by the way. I've looked everywhere. She seems to have vanished—

Into thin air? says Reagan. Very funny. You have no experience spotting birds. She gestures toward a very serious-looking set of binoculars upright on a bureau. They don't just sit at the end of a branch and flap their wings.

You've looked for her yourself?

I am paying you, snaps Reagan and shuts her eyes. I could find her myself but then I'd still need you for rehoming and nesting since she's violent.

That little gun is what she reminds him of, lying on the table about to go off. She's not the same woman he made a deal with at the Club, her mind is filled with something other than reality. One bird will attract another, he says.

She sighs. Usually a bird does return if it sees another of its flock, so perhaps your plan will work.

The second bird is aggressive, and she doesn't like me, he says.

She doesn't like me, Reagan mimics him. She draws her lips together, then clip-clops her heels over to that tote of hers across the room, where she extracts another green wad of bills. Good thing I think of all the contingencies. She holds it out to him.

He stands there; he counts it. Not very fast, but he counts it.

She sits on the edge of the couch, clasping the tote handles. It will take my lab in Switzerland a week to produce more scent. I didn't think the job would require so much. We still don't know exactly how long it will carry the egg prior to showing, let alone laying. The whole process could be very short. After all, if the bird is too heavy to fly, it will starve. She looks up from the couch, seeming to notice him for the first time. You're looking pretty birdy yourself.

He touches the feather stubble on his chin. I just need a shave.

And what about the boy you dragged along? What are you going to do with him?

Having him keeps the other bird from offing me. I'll return him afterward, say I found him wandering around out of his mind, because he is. Maybe he'll tell these weird bird stories, sure, but nobody will believe him—he's been diagnosed already as crazy. Case closed.

She looks skeptical. I see, she says. She selects a marble egg from a bowl beside the couch and turns it in her hand. What a bother, an embryo.

He mumbles: You don't care about the birds at all?

Sure, I do, she purrs, I'm president of the conservancy.

He paws through a cabinet for coffee makings. There has to be something in here. After all, it's an office building. Well, a study lab, according to the sign. But people can't study without coffee. Although he hasn't seen any sign of employees, let alone students. He, on the other hand, has to show up at the office in the morning after a long drive tonight, then drive right back after, to search again for Roxy. She must be around now that he's got Coco. He can't not return—and Reagan knows that—because Roxy's gone. He doesn't remember having so much concern about a woman or impending fatherhood before. Might be love. But this time the birth looks to be sudden and imminent and possibly awful. He can't sleep anyway. He needs coffee.

All he comes up with are the little creamers. His boy used to open piles of them at the café, drinking them down one by one just to annoy him while he annoyed his wife by waiting until the last minute to drop him off. That's before she got all fussy about his always being late, and the judge changed it to sole custody. Maybe the kid even drinks coffee himself by now. They would've played plenty of ball together at his age, taken in a game or two—no, played a lot of rounds of Grand Theft Auto, screaming at the top of their lungs after running the bad guy off the road with a zombie horde. But that ex-wife of his would've peeled his ass for more support money. He never told Roxy about him. Too much out of the past.

He tries another office, this one labeled Administration. Secretaries always have coffee. Or somebody who comes in and feeds the birds every day. Or maybe she does it herself? Boy, is he tired.

He could have rented a whole suite for the night with all the money Reagan's paid him, though he was lucky he held onto it, given that she was furious when he refused to kill Chris. That would've put him in a big bind with regard to other jobs, not to mention he's somebody's kid. Funny how she's too lazy to go down and check out Coco herself. Maybe she's too chicken, going on and on about her bite.

Just when he's beginning to think he should be happy with creamers, he finds a packet of instant in the lab, probably left behind by a construction worker because the paint looks so fresh. Only a paper cup sits at the very back of the shelf, but he fills it at this fountain next to a statue-thing of a bird so abstract it could be a winged sandwich, then tries to stir the contents of instant into the cold water and fails. Ugh. He pours some of the creamer on top of the coffee granules, then he stirs the mess with his finger and tries to suck off the wet grit.

My kid isn't crazy. My kid is good. Or, well, maybe he isn't. Maybe he's wrong about his own kid. He was wrong about Roxy. She bit Reagan just like that. Coco could finish him off if he moves to within a foot of her.

He drinks his drink.

For now, all he's going to do is not get—whatever—bitten. He eyes the tranq gun he's left on the chair, then pats the pistol he's got stuck in his waistband. There's still some birdseed in his pocket. He swallows it with the rest of the putrid coffee. Coughing on the seed, his head starts to clear.

He longs to hold Roxy again. He longs. That's really the only reason why he didn't march off in the middle of the night and quit this crazy-ass assignment. He's not in it for the pension.

Chapter 46

CHRIS BEATS on the cabinet, a battering that's ear-splitting, then he's talking talking talking, he's circling the room, one cabinet at a time, more rat-tat-tats. He stops, breathes deep. I sense he's looking at me. I open my eyes and shake my head free of the drug, and this time I wink.

Chris jumps. You're not, like dead, like a dead bird, are you?

I don't have the flu, if that's what you mean.

There's a light on in the farthest part of the house, he says, talking fast, talking faster. I saw it coming in, that's where they're questioning Roxy, that's where they're getting out the truth. She's not sick either. You're a bird.

Harpy, I say.

He keeps talking. About everything. Faster, faster.

We're here to rescue Roxy, I interrupt. She's probably already been here for a couple of days. Did you take the meds you were supposed to?

A general wanted to cross this river, he says. His soldiers

said no, it will make you forget. But the general crossed the river and then called out each of the soldiers' names to cross behind him, and they each crossed, and the general won the battle. He didn't forget any of them.

That was in Portugal, I say. I'll take your answer as a no. Chris—Chris—I interrupt again. Did you get into another fight with your dad?

Where'd you hear that? Geez, you're really not on the case. I am on the case. I said to Tim, sure, let's go somewhere, wherever, and Tim gave me a lift. You have feathers.

I wiggle my arms to life but I can't release my restraints by myself.

You're definitely a bird. Unless I'm hallucinating. I could be hallucinating. Chris gets really agitated, then he goes for the door, looking all around and behind him, and then he lunges for the table, starts tapping it. But maybe you do have the flu.

I don't, I say. My wings are killing me, but I don't go into that, he's already having a hard time. Could you find something to cut me loose?

Cool, cool, he says, but he can't. There's nothing in the room that will cut, the drawers and cupboards are empty. He rips off half a fingernail trying to break the plastic on the restraint, he chews at it and still manages to talk. I'm on the case. I will get this off. We'll find Roxy, don't you worry. You know, Tim's not the greatest. He once shouted at me in front of the office. I told you about that, didn't I? Then his voice rises: My skateboard! It's in the van!

He seriously tries the door. When it doesn't budge, he whirls around and whacks the stainless steel table hard with his hand. The sound reverberates so loud that he stops whacking for a second.

Footsteps? No footsteps.

Don't, I say. Don't do that again.

Okay, okay, he says. He holds his fingers together, but they twitch. I note how white they are, how tight he has to hold them. My board, he says again.

You're really not well.

Bipolar like the doctor said sounds like I'm two-headed and hopeless, he says. A Bip.

Two-headed means two poles, you're either up or down. Medication helps, you know that.

He can't keep from drumming, he breaks away, he touches his face all over with his fingers, he starts drumming again. His lips are purple from biting them, from trying not to talk.

What do you want to say?

Am I dreaming you? He drums. Are those really claws? He's going to do something to you, he says. I just know it.

I want to give him a hug. I can take care of myself, I tell him.

You're on the case then too. Bip, I'm a Bip. He hops from one end of the room to the other. My dad hates me all the time. He can't stand me. He ties me up.

It's hard for him to know how to protect you.

My board! He starts drumming on the table again, no

rhythm. Bip, bip, he says to his drumming. Gripping himself to control his hands, he stares out the window at the big dark trees. Your sister's a bird too, not a dealer.

You're right. And you don't really want to kill your father.

No, he says, and he goes quiet for whole seconds.

I follow his gaze. There's a window between the sink and the cupboards. It's dark out but what I know of the history of child abuse is darker: not a hundred feet away a child accused of witchcraft was lit on fire by an angry Puritan, down the trail along the back of the aviary a boy on a hunt was stripped of his clothing and beaten for running too slow, and a little farther, three children fell off an unfinished staircase and the uncle, hammer in hand, said it was an accident.

I too notice a tree with one branch bending lower than the others.

Chapter 47

TIM'S SO tired he sleeps six hours upright in the van, then it takes him a full two hours to get back to the office. He's barely clocked in when a very big homeless man blocks his door: shaved head, crumbs in his beard, stains on his shirt, pants shot, hands filthy. But Tim's probably the one who looks homeless, having not shaved for two days, and no shower. While the guy paws through a shopping bag, Tim spots a tattoo of an eagle on his neck. Another crazy?

I need to arrest one of your employees, he says. He holds up Coco's picture.

Not homeless. Tim stands on one foot, then the other. Your badge, sir?

The man is exasperated. I get no backup and now there's attitude? He produces a laminated ID in several languages.

This logo is unfamiliar to me, says Tim. You could have printed it up ten minutes ago.

Man, you're stalling. Are you really going to be sticky about this? She is very dangerous.

Listen. Tim leans over his desk. We are not in the business of hiring dangerous criminals. You'll have to bring in a warrant.

Huh, he says, like that's a statement. You're awfully familiar with the law. The man tries to stare him down, then scrolls to something on his phone. Here, he says. He pushes the phone at him.

It's a standard warrant, signed electronically.

That's how they do it these days? Anybody could fill this out, says Tim. I need paper. Like Coco, he doesn't say.

The man steps up closer. Just hand her over. Don't give me this paper shit. I'm a professional.

Tim almost nods. He guesses that anybody who says he's professional must be worried someone will find out he isn't. Excuse me, he says. I just need a hard copy and then we can proceed. The printer's in another room. If you could just press print on your phone, it'll send over—

The man takes Tim's card from its holder on the desk and squints at the number. Okay, Tim. With barely suppressed rage, he searches for the app on his phone.

Let me make sure the machine is on. I'll just be a second.

Tim marches out of the room, bypasses the printer, heads for the delivery ramp, exits through the double doors, wrenches open the van he's just parked, and pulls the key from his pocket.

He doesn't need somebody else messing with this.

Chapter 48

ROBINSON IS quite unhappy when he realizes Tim has exited social services, and he causes a scene, and one angry gesture accidentally knocks the trash in the hall to the floor. How was he to know it was full to the top with shredded files? He tries to gather up what he's spilled, he wants to get back on track by asking this Black dude a few questions before he chases Tim down. Have you seen this woman? he says, pressing the rest of the shredded paper into the bin with his knuckles, shoving his phone into the dude's face.

He's not so excited about answering. He looks at the phone and looks at him. He hesitates. Everybody knows people identify somebody in a half second. She was here a half hour ago, he says.

As Robinson is in the business of tailing her, he laughs at the lie. A couple of days ago, or maybe yesterday is more like it.

What else can he say? Or do? Robinson storms out. Calm down, he says to himself. Tim has ten minutes on him, so what? He's slapped a transponder under all three of the social service vehicles, just in case. A hunch. That's why Robinson looks so dirty, having been flat on his back on the oil stains. He drives his own van out of the parking lot slowly, a thinking maneuver. Did Tim have time to look under the chassis?

Robinson checks his tracer. It's good.

But before his first-ever car chase, he has to pick up the dog. His wife offered to have the kids come over from the shelter and walk him, but he would have had to pay them to do it, her idea. He found the dog his own job, guarding one of those barbed-wired parking lots full of new cars. It's the dog's first day. He gave him double dog food in preparation, and a new collar.

He arrives at the lot with a screech, and car lot dust. The dealer says he doesn't need to bring him in again. He practically licked a car thief to death, or so the dealer said, when he caught the guy taking off a set of plates.

Well, he's really a hunting dog, he says, gathering his pride.

That mutt? The dealer shakes his head.

In you go, Robinson says to the dog. Let's hunt.

Chapter 49

LEFT AT the plaque that says that she's one of the best conservationists in the country, right, no, left around the water fountain, and then straight ahead past the study labs to the exam room. Tim is so tired he keeps turning the wrong way. He's right in front of the aviary when he stops at the rack to collect the tranq guns again.

And this was supposed to be strictly a delivery, he mutters, cramming the smaller pistol into his back pocket where it doesn't press so hard on his gut, then works the mechanism on the rifle. Well, delivery plus. He tamps down all that love, or is it just lust he feels? After he left Coco and the boy, he was sure he'd catch Roxy, no way would she hide anymore—but no such luck. When he faces the exam room, he sticks the tranq gun under his armpit so he can slide the bolt on the door open with both hands. It's awkward.

He quick-points the gun into the room.

The boy's leaning against the side of the exam table, and

Coco looks to still be asleep in the cart, fluffy and feathery, very feminine, an odd look for her. All the boy does when he sees him is clench his jaw and start talking again, low and then fast, gibberish mostly, his face wan and pale and probably sleepless too.

Do you need the john? he asks, lowering the gun.

I can fly, says Chris in a pinched voice. No, really. She taught me how. It was last night, after she was asleep. It happened fast. I just learned. If you stand here, right here, you'll learn too. It's easy. I can do it and I don't even have wings. You just have to try.

Another text. He's had twenty texts already from that homeless-looking guy who wanted Coco, enough chimes to start a church service. If the guy's so official, why didn't he just jump in a car and follow me?

Turn around, he says to Chris. He can't believe he forgot to frisk him.

Really, you don't believe me, but I can fly. I could teach you. You thought I didn't know, I'll bet. I'm pretty smart and after she was asleep—

She's drugged, he says. But not for long. He wrenches a cell phone out of the boy's tight back pocket. You haven't been using this, have you?

Flying is almost like sleeping, says Chris. Flying keeps you awake. I love it. I love flying. I didn't dream it.

You're weird, says Tim, and checks for messages. Nothing from Roxy, a couple from the kid's father but it doesn't look as if he's answered any of them. Too crazy.

show you. The kid walks over to the French doors and starts loosening his belt.

A looney double-time, Tim says, keeping everything under control, his gun pointed at the boy, then at Coco. Get back in here.

Coco jerks forward in her cart to growl at Reagan: I want Roxy.

Reagan startles and steps away.

I know where she is, says Chris, still working at his belt. Don't you worry.

Tim fumbles with the smaller gun. He has to cover Coco too. Keep your pants on, boy, he says. Get over here.

Chris is bent at the waist, shaking a little, still talking. Just let me—

Tim shifts the tranq gun toward him, the smaller one at Coco.

I can definitely fly, he says. And I know where the bird is, don't you worry. I know, I'm crazy. He leans way over the balcony.

Honestly, says Reagan and takes a step toward Chris.

Instead of jumping off the balcony, he whips his belt around and down. A snap and a crack, and the buckle rebounds on Reagan's face, right near that bandage. She screams. He whips it again and a lamp breaks, then Tim almost gets hit.

Cut it out! Tim yells. He can't get a good bead on the kid because he's whirling around and around now, and in one crazy wild turn he almost hits the woman in the face again and she shoots—accidentally?—her little gun, the real one, up at the skylight.

The glass cracks.

Put down that belt, screams Reagan, advancing on him in siege position, the gun outstretched, her other hand over her twice-wounded cheek. She shoots again, this time at his feet.

He drops the belt just the way she tells him to. Buckle-first, it thuds to the ground.

Oh, my god, I'm going to have to move a chair over that hole, Reagan says, staring at what the bullet's done to her floor.

Coco? says a voice from above.

Roxy plunges through the skylight, feet first, in a rain of glass. Screeching tears at the air, so loud everybody but the two birds cover their ears. Roxy, already a little bulbous with egg, releases Coco from her restraints with two quick slices of her talons.

Get out of here, shrieks Coco, launching herself out of the cart. When Roxy hesitates, Coco throws herself at her, fighting and clawing and flying, feathers everywhere, Coco trying to push Roxy back up and out through the skylight's hole, both of them screeching impossibly loud.

She must have heard the shot, shouts Reagan, with a smirk on her face. Dumb bird.

You're the one who's dumb, says the kid.

Roxy's only a couple of feet over Tim's head when he shoots her. Coco turns on him and Tim pops her too with the smaller gun. It works on her just as well. They go down slowly, like leaves in a breeze, cursing at him. Roxy barely clears the broken glass and Coco lands hard against the wall. All the while the kid is screeching the way the birds were, he's running around screeching, barely holding up his pants.

I'm sorry, Tim says and snaps plastic restraints around the moaning Coco, then kneels in the glass at Roxy's side. She's out cold. I'm really sorry, he whispers. He pins her wrists and feet together.

I have a feeling that she will lay fairly quickly, says Reagan, who's summoned enough courage to stand next to him. Survival in the wild had to be efficient. It had better be—my meeting is in three days.

They hardly notice that the kid is gone.

Chapter 50

ROXY NUDGES the lint off the rug with her tongue, she mouths a button out of the cracks of the sofa that Tim has dragged in to put next to the scratching post, she finds fuzz from somewhere else and blows it together into a pile in our pretend bedroom in the aviary, such as Tim has devised. If only she had some glitter for this erstwhile nest. She does manage to kick a mound of pebbles around the edge. All of this takes her some doing, hours of concentrated effort because she and I remain in restraints, with a dog muzzle on me. They couldn't find one for Roxy but Reagan thinks the advancing pregnancy will take all the sass out of her. That may be. She can hardly move with the huge swelling now protruding from her belly. Most of the time she just stares into this little pile of a nest she's made, head cocked. She can't really add anything else. If she pulls out any more feathers, she'll have a bald patch.

You going to climb on top and sit on it?

Two more days gone already, she says.

The bulge on her is too big to be a harpy's, we both see that. If some harpy male tups the new chick when it's grown—if it's female—there's a chance those genes will realign in the next generation and a creature much more harpy will be the result. If it's a male, reproduction with humans produces sterile offspring. Half-harpy females need full-blooded harpy males. The last official sighting of a male harpy was in 2000 when someone on Facebook reported a loud owl-like sound coming from a guy in feathers perched on an English steeple.

She shrugs when I tell her this bit about Facebook, she doesn't take her eyes off the nest. Maybe you could give the chick my feather collection, she says far too calmly.

You're going to give it to her yourself, I don't say. Okay, is what I say, is the feather collection behind more stuff in the closet?

Yeah, she says. I hid it so you wouldn't be tempted to fletch any arrows or make a hat.

I could laugh or I could be sad. I know sad, that human weight, but now is not the time for either. I need to be angry. This is the Alcatraz of aviaries, glassed in all around, that hole Roxy came through boarded over in less than an hour by emergency workers. Other exotic species stuck inside with us shit on us, but at least Roxy caught one with her teeth when it flew too close. The noise at night! Reagan doesn't like to turn off the lights. People don't trust birds in the dark. Now and then Tim comes in through the barrier, the kind they use for butterfly exhibitions, to hose us down—of course there's no toilet—and to leave snacks of raw eggs, pickles for my sister, sardines, once a catfish with the head still on, and once a peanut butter smoothie with a straw for me and my muzzle, as well as woeful expressions. Or maybe leering expressions, since we're both still naked, down to our down and feathers. The aviary's a little chilly—those plastic barriers are drafty.

My sister can't take her eyes off Tim the second he shows up. No more tidbits? she asks.

He makes the most inhuman grimaces, he's so distraught.

Murderer, I hiss at him.

He takes off his shirt to show us the feathers popping out all over his shoulders, around his neck, his face, his belly, and his down. He's going farther into bird than humans have for a millennium, much farther. He strokes his chin where he's shaved off the feathers. Maybe the stroking calms him. Whatever he's used was strong, like testosterone gone wild, and his DNA has probably reverted to the primeval bird version halfway to dinosaur. My sister goes totally out of it when he visits, cluck-cluck-clucking, the combination of maternal hormones and what he gives off himself overwhelms her. I roll and hop away from the two of them as best I can.

There's really no retreat, my sister says to me after he's gone, and she puts her hand over her belly as if to protect it. Or as if it's an anchor.

I could stab you and pull the thing out.

I suppose you could, she says, avoiding my eyes in case

I'm serious. She'd be dead for sure then, bleeding is very hard to stop around the ovaries. You know, there's supposed to be another hormone in men that shows up when the off-spring appears, she says. It's called affection.

Yeah, the conflicted kind? You can trust Tim for that.

I know him better than you do.

It must be so amazing, love, that rush of desire and lust and longing. She's determined to bear this egg, especially given the outcome of the last one she laid, the one the tiger ate. I stand in my far corner, breathing in slowly, trying to check my rage. Besides Roxy's ever-growing plight, Chris is starving somewhere in the bushes or worse: picked up and committed for talking nonstop about women who are birds. I wish I could help him too. I'm furious that I can't do anything.

Tim slams his way into the aviary again. Along with his tranq gun, he's dragging several just-cut boughs and holds a fistful of cotton batting in his hand. I have to take the sofa away, Reagan's idea, he says. Not birdy enough for a nest.

What about the rug? Why doesn't she take the rug too? I taunt.

I'll leave my jacket though, he says instead of answering me. He uses its leather to mat the boughs and the cotton batting down once he gets it all arranged. This is a really good nest, he says.

How would you know? I screech.

He scoops up the pile of debris Roxy's made and drops

it into his nest. Sweetheart, he says, stroking her feathered parts flat, murmuring into her neck. He carries her over to the nest and tucks her in. She coos, she flutters, she can't get out because her belly's too heavy.

Okay, he says. You, he says to me, we're calling Stewie. He's been bothering me all afternoon and says he'll call the cops if he doesn't hear from you. He inputs the numbers and sticks the phone in my face. Watch yourself. Isn't that what they say in the movies?

Three rings.

Stewie, I say. Just returning your call.

We're frantic here. A lot of people are wondering—all three of you don't show up for work for days, a kid is gone, his father's worried sick. Stewie makes an exasperated sigh. What's the deal?

Everyone's okay, I say.

Where are you? Your place is a mess. The super let me in.

I'm nowhere really, I say in a flat voice.

Uh-huh, says Stewie and his voice softens. You know, I found a very pretty feather—

I watch a couple of rare birds bill and coo above me, I smile. Ask me about that in nine and a half years.

Tim jerks the phone away and snuffs the call. What did you mean by nine and a half years? Some kind of code?

I tell him nothing.

Leave her alone, says Roxy.

I know that tone of voice, and it isn't the man-crazy one.

I wiggle my way to standing, I will not spend another second on the ground. I want to lunge at him and rip out his throat—but I can't.

He stands soldier-stiff beside the nest. I love you, he says to her.

Shut up, shut up, shut up—she's going to be torn apart by the egg, I say.

She leans toward him, and I think she's going to do him in with her teeth, but instead she whispers something I can't hear.

You're not going to die, he says, and brandishes his gun as if that will protect her from what he's started.

Chapter 51

THE DIRT road is considerably more narrow than Robinson would like but all these glitzy secret places seem to have them this size, the rich owner's one big-car-wide, fit for no other. Mud has spattered halfway up the van, camouflage from a rainstorm on the way here. He parks it in a turnaround under a tree, rolls down the front window just enough for the dog. Although the dog did once step on the window button and get out, he's told him a thousand times no, and he hasn't done it since. He shoulders a knapsack and clips a little button camera to the back of it. He's a hiker, if anybody in the area wants to know, and it's true, there's still a mile to go before getting to the estate in question.

A whole mile. He huffs, he puffs. Too many pizzas, too much time in the van, he can barely lift his feet. He needs more exercise—he should have worked out for a week—so he could climb the citadel ahead, hand over hand, etc. It is, after all, a citadel. The building rises up like a Disney fairytale in the middle of the grounds, but the modern glassed-in addition beside it looks as if it were glued on from an entirely different toy set. He stations himself behind a tree not too far from the gate, hiding behind those fancy stone walls that look as if the squirrels put them together on their off days, and does what he does best— watches.

For hours.

Not many squirrels.

Midafternoon, two vans drive up, with something-something caterers printed on the side. He stuffs his not-so-clean shirt into the gap that has opened up in the last few weeks between his low-slung pants and the overhang of his ever-widening belly, tosses the rucksack into the bushes, clips the camera onto his polo shirt, and hustles past the automatic gate before it closes behind the vans. The head honcho of the entourage is handing out uniforms to a line of workers by the time he makes it to the parking area a hundred feet in. Like all these day jobs, outfits like this seldom know who they've hired until they show up. Or else they need help so much they don't ask.

Sorry, I'm late, he says when it's his turn for a uniform. I had to park outside.

You're a big guy, says the caterer, pawing deep into the dry-cleaning for something suitable. He hands him pants and a white jacket, the second like a tent, it's so wide. And what's that you've got on your feet?

The man points an accusing finger at his hiking boots.

What kind of idiots is the office sending me? he mutters. Tattoos and Jesus, Mary and Joseph, and all the saints in heaven. I don't want you on the floor except for clearing at the end, do you understand? You stay behind and shovel.

Shovel? What that means he doesn't have to ask, he's hungry. He folds the uniform over his arm and heads inside.

Chapter 52

A DOZEN candelabras, old wax dripped to the hand-holds—where have I seen this setup before? Bad horror movies from the fifties. A row of mirrors retrieved from the basement by the caterers reflect the candlelight infinitum and that reminds me of feathers, their rippling protective overlap. Tiki torches in sconces screwed into the walls complete the ambiance, giving the place a gauzy two-for-one look. I'm watching from high up in one of the tallest aviary trees, having escaped my bonds, courtesy of Chris. He'd been hiding all along in a faux ostrich den at the other end of the aviary, talking to the ostriches. This morning he freed my wrists through the fence with a jagged piece of sharp metal, junk forgotten by the construction crew. We're going to be fine, I lied. Chris's monologue was still in full force but drowned out most of the time by the cacophony of the disturbed birds. Take some of our food, I told him, and I gave him the crackers Tim left the last time and a jar of peanut butter. As soon as Chris was hidden again, I flew into the thickest-leaved branches.

Tim had already freed Roxy completely since the size of her egg now made flight impossible. She's started laying already, birthing the egg. The whole process, from insemination to delivery, is taking only a week. Producing this egg is killing her, and it sounds like it. It is killing me too, just to listen. Muffled screams, because, of course, she has to be gagged—can't let the caterers hear her. They're now unloading cases of wine, fancy glassware, hors d'oeuvres, and what appears to be a huge Fabergé egg decorated in ruffles and a crown, shut tight inside a glass case. Matching the décor, Reagan has changed into a gown, really more of a nightgown with drama, a white tunic with gold straps across the front—and the rip in her cheek is makeup-smeared.

Keep it up, she urges Roxy, not like a birthing coach but more as if she's worried the delivery won't happen in time for her party. She may have said other things, but my sister's agony is all I catch. If Roxy hadn't had the egg on the way, I'm sure Reagan would have removed it by force. The aviary birds go wild in sympathy and their noise on top of hers is dreadful. I'm wild too but helpless. I can't rescue Roxy or the egg, it's too dangerous for both of them. I can't do anything until the egg is out.

Soon the candelabras drip their wax past their handholds onto the tables. Their flickering in the mirrors makes it even harder for anyone to spot me. Once in a while Reagan looks up into the trees, searching while the caterers work around her. What a crescendo of fury she aimed at Tim when he confessed I was gone. You couldn't keep two hens in the henhouse? She's sure I'm going to come out of nowhere after the egg appears and slash her to bits.

Yes. I. will.

Reagan herself rigs up a thick velvet curtain on poles around Roxy's nest. For privacy? So she can monitor the labor without disruption. I want so much to be down there, at least holding her hand. My poor sister! I remember too well—with horror—my mother's deathly struggle. Roxy should have been there too, I realize now. Instead, I'd sent her to a quiet convent for six months, but seeing my mother so damaged might have prevented her from succumbing to Tim. The human chick of my mother's didn't last that long anyway, it was the fifteenth century, lifespan forty years. Roxy's been safe all this time, despite the acculturation that's slowly erasing our differences with humans. I feel adrenaline rushing through me, I'm getting more and more enraged at Tim, at the whole human race, but even worse, at myself. I simply should have dragged her off, moaning and weeping, to Europe.

Tim has staked out a place to watch for me, with binoculars to his face every three minutes and both ridiculous guns at his side. My sister's muffled screams unnerve him, and the other birds are screaming back. He's starting to shake, which makes staring into the binoculars even harder.

No sign of Chris. Has he gone for help? Does he need help? I'm stuck in my camouflage for now. He has managed to take care of himself for a few days—it won't be much longer.

Reagan begins hooking up some kind of apparatus beside the nest. I don't like the look of it, a suction device with a hose ending in a needle point. Behind it, a display case has been made ready for the egg, with wooden holders to cradle it upright, and a lock on its door. Reagan fusses with the nest, filling the cracks with what looks like plastic foam, more "realistic" I guess, and a spray of flowers to hide the blood already leaking from Roxy. Roxy hisses at her, but she's weak and by now Reagan knows to stay away. Finished with her beautification project, she leans back and stares at the foliage, searching for me again.

Humans are not natural lookers. Their attention is usually on each other, so they don't see a situation the way a bird might, we who are "two eyes with wings." I'm hanging upside down from a branch in the thickest part of her fake forest, my back killing me from trying to sleep on the boughs. And they used to be so comfortable three thousand years ago! All anyone can see is a dark scruff, if that, as my forehead matches the cement of the balcony behind me. But I'm no bat with one-way blood circulation. Chickens held upside down, for example, get stupid. Basically, they start to suffocate.

Tim drops the binoculars with a crash, having collapsed with no sleep. Reagan lays into him.

I creep to a higher perch where I can better see the whole aviary, and I wait.

Chapter 53

I'M ALERT when men—mostly men—driving good cars, and a few beat-up but classy pickups, pull up to the portico after dark, and ring the bell. They come wearing club drag: cummerbund, satin-lapeled jackets and striped pants, one of them in a top hat and tails. The few women who get out of the cars look drab in dark cocktail dresses. They shed their cell phones and devices in a basket in front of Tim who's wearing a button on his T-shirt that says *Security*, then parade into the aviary, oohing and aahing at its construction, and at each other. One of the guests hoots like an owl in greeting, one of them tucks his hands into his armpits and flaps, one of them demonstrates the latest egg vest. He holds it open whenever asked, as if he's selling stolen watches. Boisterous laughter breaks out when one of them manages to identify his stash of four tiny eggs in Latin. Ten thousand of these, he boasts, that's how many I smuggled out of an English museum in a tricked-out wheelchair. They seem oblivious of the possibility of bird droppings from above or attacks. Birds are their friends! Their suppliers! By this time, the caterers are making a second round with the wine.

With the curtain in front of Roxy so thick, nobody seems to hear my sister moaning and straining and crying over their own bird calls and the aviary's birds, but I can hear my sister's gasps quite clearly. My wings quiver with pent-up violence.

Eventually the guests gather for toasts around the candelabra-strewn tables.

Let us drink to our chairman, begins the man who has placed his top hat on the chair beside him. To Reagan. At the opposite end, she bows in acknowledgment. There is applause and glasses are raised. Hear, hear. There are many reasons for our obsession, as many as there are members, the man continues. The members look wise at this point. The wine is taking effect, making them quieter, and although the caterers are still bustling around, surely they can hear my sister now, her increased agony building tension in the room. But it's not *Help, help*, it's a cry that's inhuman and beyond bird.

He keeps talking. There are those whose interests are in zoology and everything animal: fur, fangs, and footprints. We are not they. Well, some of us are, even employed by the great universities.

A couple of the men nod their heads ever so slightly, and everyone drinks to that.

There are those who deeply care about birds in particular.

But we are not they either. Birds are just vehicles to us. Flights of fancy against the azure sky.

Vehicles, call out several from the crowd.

Freud would say we had issues, unresolved, from our childhood. Clearly from our mothers, but maybe even our fathers, who threatened eggs metaphorically, symbolically, who took great pains to eviscerate the poached innards with spoon and thumb, who were happiest when the back of a knife sundered the egg, shattering it into two. Crack, they would say, with relish. And we would weep.

The audience taps their spoons to the table in appreciation, and drinks again.

Yet there are others who became eggers without such consolations or terrors, for example our chairperson, who inherited her mother's vast understanding of all things avian, and known for decades as the "Empress of the Avians." Now, in response, the daughter has outdone the empress herself in her own unrelenting quest to acquire the world's rarest egg.

His pause is dramatic and fills with applause.

Reagan grimaces with the exquisite pleasure of recognition. The guests raise their glasses again and she takes over: Gentlemen and gentlewomen, oologists all. As you know, I have made an amazing discovery, one that far surpasses my previous, which, as of course you remember, was the delivery of the very last intact egg of the dodo.

They make a weird sound in unison as if they are all dodos, as if they know how a dodo is supposed to sound.

Nobody has seen or heard a dodo for centuries. I can't tell whether they are all pulling each other's legs, but the call is not right, it's way off. And, of course, they drink to it.

This dodo egg, she says, when they quiet, has been, until now, the crowning piece of my collection. Let me show it to you again. She walks over to the middle of the table, and unlocks the glass-fronted case, revealing the dodo egg nestled inside, dolled up Fabergé-style. She removes the egg and turns to her audience to show it off, holding it aloft to more applause.

Oh my god, shrieks one of the women. How beautiful.

From my vantage, that's no dodo egg. I've seen actual live dodos lay eggs and they could never have laid an egg the size of the one on the table. Elephant bird? Maybe. There is a museum in South Africa that's trying the same ruse, a famous scientist claiming to have inherited a dodo egg from an ancient Dutch ancestor. The bigger the egg, the bigger the legend.

She locks the presumed dodo egg back into its case. Now, will the staff please remove themselves?

When the caterers abandon their positions at the back of the aviary and file through the door, I notice, from my bird's-eye-perch, one of the biggest of them has a tattoo of an eagle on the back of his neck. I don't have time to contemplate this turn of events. Tim has reappeared waving his tranq gun, poking at the trees with its barrel. Very unconvincing. The audience goes dead quiet anyway. In the midst of this, my sister screams her worst. Okay—she squawks, finally ungagged, she squawks very, very loudly. Don't worry, Reagan announces. It's all part of the presentation. She throws open the curtain with a flourish.

Roxy's egg, three times bigger than the supposed dodo that's just been displayed, lies at her feet, sky-blue and mottled with brown, the shell translucent. You can almost see the something inside stirring. Reagan rolls it away from Roxy, who has fallen back on her haunches, gray and drawn. Bleeding? I can't tell. Certainly she's shivering, her wings crumpled behind her, her talons withdrawn. Reagan heaves the egg high, the trophy streaked with blood. For a moment I think she's going to dash it to the floor. All applaud, except Tim, whose gun isn't pointed into the aviary anymore but dangles toward the floor as he steps toward the moaning Roxy. Reagan doesn't notice, she's absorbed in her moment of triumph; she's carefully placing the new egg on the red velvet inside the case so secure on its pedestal, then locking it shut with a snap. Now the applause is deafening, the audience has risen to its feet.

Tim is kneeling beside Roxy, gun on the floor, while Reagan swings the needle coupling into position, readying it to pierce the egg.

No.

I expand my wings to their full size, far larger than what humans imagine, and I shriek. That's what one animal does to another to intimidate. I shriek and I gather my strength, and with one great long swoop, I dive down and put out most of the candles with the ferocity of a single flap.

Reagan and her colleagues cower, except Tim, who quickly swings his gun into the air.

I could quarter him like a lamb for the barbecue. But since he seems to actually love my sister and she feels something for him, and since that isn't a real gun for whatever reason, it is enough that I plummet down and slash deep into his arm, the one shaking, the gun barely aimed.

He drops it entirely.

Through the chaos of the fleeing fellow clubbies, Reagan fires at me with her pistol. She shoots twice—the aviary glass rains down again—and wings me. I suppose it would be great for her if she could capture me alive, but not much less fame if I am dead.

I can still swoop with a hit wing, and I do. I scatter whoever's left at the table and summon all my strength to soar straight down at her, grabbing at her strap. Pumping my good wing as hard as I can, I cantilever her weight with my bad one and lift her high, higher, right to the top of the aviary.

People scream below. Reagan is screaming. It's very noisy, it's annoyingly noisy and she's heavy and hard to hold with one hand while she's screaming.

I could kill her, of course, but I choose to let the punishment fit the crime. Since she wanted so much to empty the eggshell, I empty hers.

Her head is what hits the table and overturns two candelabras.

She won't remember much of anything when she comes

to. It's her snake brain I've wiped out with my calculated drop, the one that starts at the back of her neck, the one that remembers its dinosaur days that we're all descendants of, not just harpies. A bad concussion for sure. Will she even have enough brain matter left to call the police?

Chapter 54

BUT FIRST I'm going to destroy every one of the megalo-maniac eggers before they can get away, and they all know it. My teeth show big, both my wings spread wide, claws flexed, and I'm hissing with fury. Below me, the clubbies scramble one over the other in the flickering dark, feet to stomach, pushing the weaker to the floor, slamming doors and emergency exits. Nobody bothers the discarded silly-looking tranq guns, so intent they are on the exits.

The egg's locked in its case. Good.

Despite his gashed arm, Tim has Roxy and her nest in his grip and is turning away from the elevator—is it jammed?—to struggle with the door to the stairs.

I turn my back on the crazed clubbies. They can punish themselves, I don't have time. I jerk the door open for Tim, blood from my wing streaking my feathers, the stairs soon slick with blood from Roxy and Tim as he heaves himself and his burden up, step by step. Where do you think you are going? I yell. I'm calling 911. Put her down.

Tim doesn't seem to hear or even see me. While I dial, fluttering to keep up, he leans over to catch something Roxy is whispering. All right, he says. Yes. Continuing to ignore me, he keeps trudging and stumbling upward as fast as he can. Roxy, Roxy, I plead but Roxy doesn't answer either. Has she fallen unconscious? Since Tim's determined to make it to the top, I fly ahead and unlatch the door but that's where Roxy says stop, and touches both of us with her hands. They're cold, she's cold. Then she closes her eyes.

No, says Tim. He manages to pull her and the nest through the door and out onto the rooftop, but it's too late, she's dead.

It can't be.

Tim extracts her from the nest, clutches her to him, and weeps full out.

I push myself between them to hold her too, and he founders backward. He starts to sob and then I sob and we stand like that, sobbing with her body propped up between us. My sister, my gorgeous sister, my confidante forever, the woman who made sense of me, who made everywhere a dovecote, who mothered me—no, sistered me when there was no mother—dead of love just like Mom? I failed to protect her, the only charge I had.

Sirens in the distance.

He pulls out a lighter. Before I can stop him, he's lit the nest at our feet on fire, all that flammable foam Reagan stuffed it with, catching with a big *whomp* of flame.

And Roxy. He drags her onto it.

I try to grab her out by the wing before she catches, and he shoves me away hard. The flames are too high in seconds for me to do anything but throw myself in after her. I don't. Through the crackle and hiss—Roxy!—hope crosses Tim's face—and then I understand. Their escape to the roof gave him hope of resurrection, a phoenix return. She must have really loved him. That—and she knew all the evidence had to be destroyed.

How quickly her remains disappear. All those tiny bones.

Tim cries out in disappointment—where's the gorgeous span of gaudy wings rising out of the smoke that he pokes his fingers through? Harpies, like people, are not immortal. The closest we get is just the usual—mother after mother after mother.

Ambulance doors slam, and someone, spotting the smoke, calls for firefighters on a walkie-talkie.

What else did she tell you? I ask Tim over what's fast becoming embers.

That you're supposed to take the egg, he says, choking back tears. He's really distraught, his eyes dart, his hands jerk. Somehow he eases his jacket off over his injury, and drops it to his feet.

He has wings now, but not very big, and they droop around his back. What the fuck? he says, not so much about what's happened to him and his body but aimed at me. He wants to prove to me that he's more than the shit that he is, killing her, kidnapping us, he wants to show me he's a real bird, a harpy, and he steps over the railing.

He can flutter, but not fly.

Reagan, sprawled at an odd angle on the banquet table, tries to talk to the ambulance people. She gestures toward the egg case with her gun. One of the medics ignores her half-finished sentences and wrings it from her hand. She groans, her fingers flex. The head caterer, scrambling to collect what's left of their equipment, tosses it into a basket of silverware. It's only after the firemen clamber to the roof to soak the burnt nest and the force of the water sprays anything left of my sister over the side, that someone peers over the back of the building and spots Tim.

I've flown to a perch in a tree just outside the aviary, with a view through its broken glass. I'm faint, having lost more blood. I hold my wing tight to my shoulder to slow its flow. The police are questioning Reagan, who's now gurgling, staring fixedly at where the egg should be. Because the egg is gone, the glass case shattered. She's wealthy enough that the police will spend some time with her, but it's a rural force, and they don't have twenty officers to cover all the exits. The egg is gone. She liked her exits, and the confusion caused by the mirrors, but now she's broken too. The egg is gone. The police can't imagine what's missing. They have their hands full with a couple of the caterers who are babbling away about a very big bird that was human. The egg is gone. A departing fireman says to check what they were drinking.

The egg is gone.

I drop down from my perch through the broken glass the minute Reagan's taken out by a phalanx of paramedics. My camouflage is the smoke from the tiki torches that have just guttered en masse. I twist a tablecloth into a toga. What will I say to a cop if he spots me—*Just out of the shower?* Luckily, Reagan has now begun to shriek while the medics pack her into the ambulance, and the head of the catering crew is smashing a pitcher because the cop doesn't believe she's seen a human bird. I start down the corridor from the aviary to the exam room where I left my clothes, where Chris and I were held that first night. Chris. I'll get to him as soon as I'm dressed. I walk fast, not looking over my shoulder. A few steps past the bird statue, I hear someone behind me. No footsteps, but someone, I'm sure.

I have to turn around.

It's Stewie. He's pounding his wings to keep his feet off the floor. Shshshshsh.

I resist running into his arms. He is like the sun in all its glory with his orange hoodie and dark wings. Where's the egg?

He doesn't know. We retrieve my clothes and he helps me jacket myself tight so the bleeding from my wing stops. He says he'll search the grounds, his eyes are pretty good. Maybe one of the eggers stowed it in a leftover box and abandoned it while running to his vehicle to escape the police. He doesn't say someone might have dropped the egg, or stolen it. Not to worry, he says. We'll find it.

I push open the door to the outside. How'd you find me?

The police traced you from your cell that time I called, but it took this long to convince them you were kidnapped and didn't, just, you know, fly away.

He smiles a wacky Stewie smile and unfurls his wings again: it's a glorious sight: big, funky shredded-at-the-tips air power—then he's gone, straight up.

Of course.

I try to stay calm about the egg, and not get wild, the bird I was before. Wild will make me a target. The only place I can't search is inside the aviary, where the police are still poking around. At least they won't notice Stewie a thousand feet up. But I can't not go to the aviary. I must find the egg before they do. I must find Chris.

Right after I pass the bird sculpture again, there's Robinson's dog, stock still, paw up, tail up, nose up, in perfect pointer position.

Give me a break.

A second later, Robinson runs up behind him.

What are you doing here? he says to the dog, and sees me. Oh, a bird.

I could flee. Instead, I put my hands up to my mouth as if I'm terrorized and rush past him for the aviary, the dog going crazy with barking. It takes Robinson a second to process my bravado, but then he's after me.

A *do-not-cross* tape is stretched across the aviary entrance, instead of a guard. I don't rip it down, I turn to face Robinson at the tape, stopping him short. He nearly pokes me in the stomach with the gun he's pulled—the one swept into the caterer's basket? Hey, I say, did you set up the chicken-footed woman?

His face contracts into a tiny grin, really a grimace of pride. My wife. She scared you?

Not really, I say. I assume there's a reward for me?

My sanity, he says.

I shrug off my jacket.

The hand he's holding the gun in starts to tremble. Keep your clothes on. I know all about how dangerous you are. Just keep walking, he says. Or I'll call the dog. Trafficking children, he says with disgust.

I burst into laughter. I'm amazed, I say. You really are brave. Swatting the gun with a talon so it hits the wall and skitters away, I hook him by the back of his coat and lift him off the ground.

Bingo! he calls frantically. Help, help!

Where's Bingo? Bingo doesn't seem to know his name.

We go high up into the aviary, where, practically single-winged, I flap through the treetops. I'm stronger when I'm angry, but I'm sad too—is this my fate, to be chased by humans all my life, and lose my sister, my mother to them? I start to shake him. First the tiny camera clipped to his collar falls to the ground, then, with another shake, out falls a zip-lock of security chips he had clutched in his hand. Then I flap a little higher to the very top where I sit on a tree and dangle him over a bough, his dog at last barking beneath us.

Put me down now, he screams, clawing for the nearby branches.

I've been trying to help your wife. How old are your kids?

They're step kids for Chrissake.

Come on. I shake him.

The little one's about two, the boy is six and the girl five.

Which is your favorite?

He doesn't say. I shake him again.

I like them all.

I slowly descend, wings flared, and set him down gently. You couldn't imagine him weighing anything he runs out of there so fast, his dog with its tail between its legs.

The police don't think to search the ostrich den, thank god.

I hiss in its direction. The ostriches beat a quick retreat. I hiss again, closer.

Chris crawls out, pulling his skateboard after him. He's talking even faster, saying how much he hates us for screwing with his board—it got scratched when he had to break the window with his belt to get into the van.

Hold on, hold on, I say.

He looks up at me, his face filthy and drawn. My dad didn't beat me, he says. I made that up.

True, I say, and then he goes on.

The kid is sore about missing the fight and all the

gunplay he heard, just like when that woman shot up that room, he says. I suppose, he says, I have to fix everything again myself now that you two messed things up?

Thank you again for that whip trick. I catch him by his shoulders. I tell him he looks as if he's been eating berries from the bushes.

I like berries, he says, holding up his hands to show his black, filthy nails. I ate the food you gave me too, he says. When do we leave?

Roxy is dead, I tell him. He stops talking abruptly, he goes down, down, away from the manic and deep into depression right in front of me, that fast. I don't console him, I'm crazy with anger and sadness, all things human, all humans, I say: You're the son of your father, whatever bad things your father or mother do to you, you will do unto others.

He says: What?

I soften. You have to crack the cycle. Take your meds. Otherwise, genes and everybody else will call the shots, and they won't forgive you anything.

He bends to his skateboard, he rolls a wheel with his fingertips, he mounts it, he barely moves in the mulch that covers the floor, he quivers. Can't you adopt me? he asks. My mom left us; she didn't die. It takes a good three minutes for him to say this, he's suddenly so slow in his instant depression. She left one day while I was at school. That's why I hate school, I'm afraid my dad will—

He motions in the air with his hands at the words he

can't say. I was too much for my mom. I failed at being her kid.

I don't have time to register my sadness with regard to that. Nobody fails at being a kid, I say. I hug him hard but what I whisper into his ear is: The egg! I need the egg. Where is it?

He scuttles back into the den and drags out the red velvet from the display case, now wrapped around the egg. I used my belt again to break the glass around it. It was hard not to break the egg too.

I don't even think about that. Thank you for all your good work, I say. I press the egg close to me. It's warm, it's heavy—

The shell is really delicate, he says. Be careful.

No, the egg is really tough.

Look—he points—already there's a crack in it and I didn't do it.

I run my finger over the fissure. It's just the chick doing some planning.

Chapter 55

MY SISTER is dead because she made a human choice, so often irrational. My sister is dead.

At least we have the egg, says Stewie.

I nod, weeping so much I cough on the tears streaming down my face. Stewie's driving us back, Chris asleep in the backseat, the egg in my lap. The trees, veiled in spring green all along the highway, form a tunnel for my grief.

I want to have nothing to do with humans ever again, nothing, I wail.

You have to care for the chick when it hatches, says Stewie, but gently, so gently.

I look out the window at the blurry green. Maybe I can raise it as a nonflying harpy, a human just living in a tree.

Stewie takes his eyes off the road and looks right at me: Get real, he says. You have to do what's best for the bird.

A song erupts from me as he drives along, despite Chris being in the car. I can't help it. My wing wants to cover my head too, but I have to sing now, right now. That swan that comes unmute after her mate's death? Ducks too. The mother penguin keening, trying to nudge a frozen chick under her body. Flocks of crows cawing, sometimes hundreds, walking around a crow corpse for as long as twenty minutes. Why anthropomorphize when it's just plain mourning?

Stewie pats my hand.

Chris snores through my singing. He must not have slept for days.

Death is even worse when it's one of your own flock, I say to him. A weight in the heart, a heaviness in flight that could take you down.

Stewie nods.

He wakes Chris when we get to his dad's place. I don't ask him what he'll tell his father about all the time he was gone and why he looks so dirty and feral. Chris is like any adolescent with a lot of problems, good with excuses. With all the various shocks he's endured in the last twenty-four hours, maybe the polar halves of his brain will make new and better connections. That's what they hoped in the 1950s when they first used electricity on the brain. Talk about a clumsy method. After electroshock, many people went back to their animal selves, still wearing their humanness as if in costume, blank and confused. But sometimes it works.

You can get screwed up with a parent, either of them,

says Stewie to Chris as he lets him out. His mom must not have been so bad because he answers: You can get screwed up without one too.

The club members don't talk to the cops. After all, they're smugglers and thieves. A few are caught fleeing the property but say nothing about any bird women, not a word about a very rare specimen on the loose. It's bad enough that all kinds of strange bird life has escaped into the area, terrifying the neighbors. Reagan is suitably confined at the hospital while the police look into her involvement in the club and its denizens. Very quickly, the membership at the Club evaporates, taking every egg that can be found on its shelves, leaving behind only a few of the less-than-perfect, the cracked and the spoiled, several heartwarming dioramas of chicks and mother hens, the more worm-eaten stuffed bird specimens that Reagan was going to discard anyway, and the remains. Out in the country, the rarer species are caught wandering or pecking at windows and are nursed back to health by Audubon volunteers, angry about their neglect throughout the investigation. Only one volunteer is injured by the spurs of an equally angry ostrich.

The Collins case, however, is not closed. The killer remains at large. If indeed, they were murdered. The police have begun to think it was some kind of weird suicide. Couple jumps from plane, holding hands. That solution is just intriguing enough that they haven't consigned the case to the cold file.

Time to move on. Again. Robinson with his stake-outs, his cameras and lens tech, came way too close. I can barely lift my wing at the moment—where did I find the strength to fly that guy high enough to scare him? Did I make a mistake not dropping him? Pity is seldom reciprocal. At least the van has moved. If anyone believes him and his footage, interest in us will surely increase. I would retreat all the way to Asia if I thought I could dodge the surveillance, not to mention the charm-makers, the shamans who trade for the shells of ostriches and the horns of hippos and the tusks of narwhals—and our feathers—to make aphrodisiacs.

But enough with the sex. With the white van at least temporarily gone, I've set up a giant incubator in our living room, a great improvement over my attempts to sit on it. Although my body temperature is perfect, I just don't have the architecture for such a big job. A large egg hatches quickly, thank god, because all the detailing has already been done in utero. Now mobile, I start to pack, throwing out Roxy's hoardings: birdcages "liberated" from Home Depot, Tesla's mash note to his pigeon (he lived with one at the Hotel New Yorker), a drawerful of old bird calendars, a package of rhinestone-studded birdy clothespins. There's pretty much nothing that can't use a rhinestone, protested Roxy when I first threatened to throw them out. Now it's hardly a victory.

Seriously, where will I fly after my wing heals? Stewie's being promoted to Tim's job but he can't have me around with my history of problems. Is Antarctica with its dying emperor penguins far enough away? That's no place to raise anyone without their feathers, and I don't think I could manage somewhere so environmentally sad and not to mention rugged anymore. I can't decide right now, I can only think about what happened to my sister, that tragedy.

I'm wondering what to think about anything when I hear the egg crack along the tiny fissure that formed when Chris kept it with the ostriches. I rush to the end of the couch where I have the egg incubating to see—

It's odd, the only time the creature inside looks old is when it's freshly hatched. Wrinkled like a suit straight out of the suitcase, kind of greasy-looking with whatever it is that makes staying inside the shell so comfortable, the new one breaks her way out by putting her fist through the shell and then her head. She shakes it—a blonde!—so the hair's less wet and shrieks something that sounds, of course, a lot like her mother.

Chapter 56

THE ONLY people legitimately wandering around in the 11 p.m. dark of the park—dog walkers—notice a prickling of movement over the tops of trees when their dogs stop to sniff then lift their heads, and they lift their heads too, in wonder. A ripple of disquiet runs through the cages at the zoo, from hiss to low roar, and the zoo guard, playing both sides of the chess board, topples the piece he's been fondling. The last gaucho in Argentina, out for a midnight ride, notices a very speedy cloud crossing the moon. Or is it a very big goose? A Spielberg cyclist? An astronomer in Iceland says it's the moon illusion, a problem in perception, whoever's watching the moon has nothing to measure the image against, and let's have another glass of *Brennevin*. Two women on a cruise down the Danube fall in love putting forward their ideas as to what they've seen in the water's reflection, reducing the two of them to hysterical nervous laughter. Taiwan and Dahomey for once have something in common: sorcerers in diesel-stinking back alleys who promise cures for infertility if someone can name what they've seen in the sky that night. And a certain skateboard shifts and falls to the floor because of some very subtle activity miles out of town that causes a boy to sit up in bed and blink.

I had little hope that very many of us would show up. After all, the males' propensity to fly into windows at the first sight of an exposed limb has been lethal with the prevalence of thermopane. But on the appointed night, harpies fly out of the woodwork, they glide in from the commuter trains and the back doors of office buildings and faraway yurts, they wing their way in formation straight to Reagan's aviary, the logical choice for a party location: the police tape still taut, its relative seclusion, the birdy amenities. To my great astonishment, the aviary is soon quite crowded. More and more harpies land, female and male, sometimes even together. How can there possibly be so many in the world? Who would've guessed?

Vive la harpy!

We weren't nearly as extinct as we feared because we finally perfected our camouflage, even from each other. Bankers and trapeze artists show, using to good stead the fearlessness that comes from thumbing gravity, literal and metaphorical, alongside housewives and retirees who, in their caged boredom, surreptitiously fly relay races around the world, telling the babysitter or caregiver not to wait up. There's a head of state whose airports are the safest in the world, and several blind harpies who, in their ecological despair, put out their eyes rather than watch the planet disintegrate.

But first, celebration.

From my initial *Help!* regarding Roxy and everything harpy, the gathering has morphed into a kind of deb ball. I'm sticking some interesting larvae onto the outside of a big cake the ten or twelve hatchlings are sharing for their various birthdays that have occurred since the last meetup. Since Tim had evolved so far, my hatchling is surely more than half and qualifies to be one of those debs. I've hidden a disgusting bird treat in the very middle of the cake that only the hardcore will eat, if hardcore exists anymore. But first, my hatchling and her peers are busy cracking the Doberman pinscher piñata with baseball bats. Bang! Out flies a ton of birdseed and there's the concomitant scramble for the macadamia nuts, then somebody starts screeching away on the karaoke. I wave at Stewie who's fooling with the sound equipment, and he waves back like a house afire, he's got a smile from here to here.

Soon a little bird steps up to the mike, her long dress dragging. Too big for her, but she had to have it. Ladies and gents, birds-all, she says. She's already drunk the bird fizzy, you can tell by how the cup in her hand dips and spills. She croons: I'm the future, pussycats.

Cringing laughter. O, irony.

She goes on to tell them about humans and harpies, how they can help each other.

Pretty great, isn't she? Stewie says, watching her descend from the podium in her four-inch heels.

I shake my head at the heels. No wonder she said the scavenger hunt would be too dangerous. And I thought it was because there are cats in the neighborhood.

She turns out to be pretty well endowed, genetically speaking, a little wobbly on her swoops and she'll never wing straight up, but she has the stamina of her cousins. She'll be a stronger, more compassionate human with the harpy part, which is what she was talking about in her speech, that bittersweet trade-off for further diluting our immortality.

We elders start the debates that make up our main contribution to the festivities. Social services isn't enough anymore, all of us agree. Direct intervention? What about the environment? Harpies are good at dropping loads from a height—could bombing the glaciers staunch the ice melt? The real key to the world's problem both behavioral and environmental is overpopulation. Maybe we should put something in the drinking water. Already it's full of sedatives and laxatives and four kinds of plastic—they'd never notice a little saltpeter.

Outer space contretemps ought to discourage their flying obsession, says one bird who focused a telescope for Galileo. Really, they need to clean up their own skies. We argue the perennial question: how long do you wait before you push a hatchling out of the nest? So many feel abandonment is at the crux of the whole human/bird dilemma.

"Cockatiels" are passed, a drink so human, so bird. Somebody's brought my favorite Fats Waller recording and a jazzy bird caller, and we start dancing and whipping our wings around. The building is sprinklered so when I brush the ceiling, the birds flutter through the downpour with glee, so dusty from flying from Columbia and New Zealand and Botswana.

Hope is a thing with feathers, sings Stewie, his tie-dye glowing in the dark.

Birds sing come rain or shine, gale or storm, I sing back. Problem is, I say, dropping my voice, we love humans.

Love? says Stewie, is funky, and he gives me a peck on the cheek.

Never discount us.

Acknowledgments

Big thanks to the following marvelous readers of *Roxy and Coco* (which appeared as *Harpies*): Marilyn Callahan, Stephanie Strickland, Steve Bull, Gay Walley, Katherine Arnoldi, Dawn Raffel, Eleanor Wilner, Molly Giles, Kara Linstrom, Margaret Laxton, Kim Young, Laura Trunkey, Roberta Allen, and an evening with the Columbia writing group. The book began at Yaddo in 2011, traveled to a retreat in Paros, Greece, where a glass of water crashed the computer, then a Ouija board had ideas at the James Merrill House, back to Yaddo for a total rewrite, on to Hawthornden in Scotland through the rain, a week in a lighthouse on Swan Island, the Betsy in Miami, and two weeks at the Hermitage. My agent, Margaret Sutherland Brown, did not give up. Much inspiration from "Operation Easter" by Julian Rubenstein in the *New Yorker*, July 22, 2013. Details about the clients of social services are true but composite. Bravo, Sarah Munroe and West Virginia University Press.